# The Art and Science of Love

Cover photo by Jozef Klopacka.
Licensed from Shutterstock.com, ID: 675590803. Used by permission.

Design by Nathan Everett

Elder Road Books Signature Edition
ISBN 978-1-955874-99-1

DISCLAIMER: This book contains content of an adult nature. This includes explicit sexual content and characters who may not conform to your religious, political, or world view. The content is inappropriate and in some cases illegal for readers under the age of 18.

# Planned 2025 Signature Collection Releases

*Soulmates,* February 2025. D.R. Peters, 'Doc' to his friends, is an artist. He paints portraits of women. Doc loves women. Many of the women he paints love him. Then smart and sexy Rita, his next door neighbor, asks him to teach her the art of love, which Doc is all too happy to do. He's not quite so sure, though when Rita, a research scientist, decides to start experimenting with the effect his relationship with his models has on his art. Doc is about to learn all about the science of the art of love.

*The Art and Science of Love,* March 2025. D.R. Peters, 'Doc' to his friends, is an artist. He paints portraits of women. Doc loves women. Many of the women he paints love him. Then smart and sexy Rita, his next door neighbor, asks him to teach her the art of love, which Doc is all too happy to do. He's not quite so sure, though when Rita, a research scientist, decides to start experimenting with the effect his relationship with his models has on his art. Doc is about to learn all about the science of the art of love.

*Drawing on the Dark Side of the Brain.* Artist Jett Blackburn's paintings reveal the soul of his subjects. They have the power to change the viewer, the model, and the artist. Sometimes emotionally, sometimes terminally. Join this digital native and his accumulation of girlfriends as they break the ties with their parents and move off to college and self-discovery.

*Strange Art.* Words just don't come easily to Art Étrange, if they come at all. His slow speech, self-consciousness, and shyness all combine to keep him isolated from his peers. He can only let his frustrations out on canvas. If it wasn't for his sister, Morgan, Art would not have survived school, but her love holds Art together through his toughest times and expands his horizons. This special Signature Collection Edition contains all three Strange Art books, *Art Something, Art Project,* and *Art Critic.*

*Bedtime Stories for Grownups.* A collection of short novellas, perfect for night time reading. "100 V Days," "My Sex Slave," "Carousel," "My Brother Reads Incest Porn. zOMG He Writes It!" and for the first public release since winning third prize in the SOL 2024 Halloween contest, "The Key to Eve."

*Schedule and Releases **Subject to Change***

# The Art and Science of Love

## Devon Layne

ELDER ROAD BOOKS
LYNNWOOD WA

# 1
# Archetypes

I FELL ON MY ass when the weed finally came loose from the rock-hard ground I call a garden. Dirt scattered everywhere, including on me. I don't know why I can't grow anything safe for human consumption, or even pleasing to the eye.

Rita drove in next door as I stood swearing at weeds, rose thorns, and the dirt in my eye. I waved as she got out of her car. I'd known Rita since she was little. Now in her mid-twenties, she was the very picture of loveliness, even dressed in a track suit boasting the name of a color across her ass.

She was a beautiful girl who had often been at my house during the summer months years ago—along with her little sister and all the rest of the neighborhood kids. They seemed to migrate from house to house, eating indiscriminately from everyone's pantry. She'd never been more to me than the neighbor kid until my sudden awakening her senior year in high school. She was a cheerleader and one day the squad went door-to-door selling candy bars to raise money for new pompoms or some such. She showed up at my front door in a pair of hot pants that showed her butt ledge and a tube top about as wide as an elastic bandage with her headlights on high beam.

"Want to support our cheer squad by buying some candy?" she asked. I hadn't realized what a sexy and provocative young woman she'd become. I nearly told her I'd like two handfuls, but I settled for buying a candy bar and then went inside for a waking wet dream.

What a fresh bit of candy was living next door.

In spite of that little episode, I managed to rein in my libido and maintained a pleasant and platonic relationship with my neighbors. Rita left for college, graduated, and got a good job as a research assistant in a science lab of some sort. She'd moved back home with her grandmother this summer to plan her fall wedding.

I called cheerfully to her as she got out of the car and she smiled and waved back.

"How's the job going?" I asked.

"Fine," she answered.

"And the wedding plans?"

I was not prepared for the sudden outburst and rush at me.

"It's been postponed… indefinitely," she said as she burst into tears.

She fell on my shoulder crying, tears soaking through my gardening shirt. She had a softness about her I couldn't help but notice as she pressed into me—a girl in sweats and, if I had to guess, nothing else. I gently led her into the house, grabbed a tissue and dabbed at her eyes as she sank into the living room sofa.

"Let's get you a cup of tea and you can tell old Doc all about it," I said. I went to the kitchen to set water on the stove to boil.

"It's awful, Doc," she whimpered behind me. "It's like I don't even know him. He's being so mean."

I'm not really a doctor, by the way—or old. Dimitri Rafael Petrovich according to my birth certificate, but I changed the last name to Peters as soon as I turned 16. I went by my initials, D.R., and kids had been calling me Doc since grade school. Like the famous Dr. Science, I'm not a real doctor. I have a master's degree… in art. That's why I make a living selling real estate.

I set the freshly brewed tea on the breakfast bar where she'd moved as soon as I went into the kitchen. Apparently, she didn't want to be alone, even in the next room. She took a sip of the tea and I waited without prompting her. Her lower lip quivered and she spoke to the teacup and not to me.

"He said I couldn't suck water from a firehose," she whimpered. "He said I just don't turn him on."

No matter what my fantasies, I certainly never expected to be privy to this kind of information. Instead of speaking, I just reached over and patted her hand. This wasn't a subject that would benefit from me prying into what she didn't want to say. It turned out, she wanted to say a lot.

"I don't know what he's complaining about. He can't say I don't turn him on. He's hard every time he walks into the room. He shoves it in my mouth and then wants to fuck. He finishes and goes to sleep, or jerks off until he's ready to fuck again. How can he say things like that? Aren't I pretty enough?"

She was steaming. Now it was time to reach in with the reassurance.

"Rita," I said gently. "You are beautiful and sexy. The guy must be an idiot."

"But why would he say I don't turn him on? I do anything he wants me to."

"Hmm. Well, let's get some things straight," I said. "It's not your problem. It's his. I hate to say it, but he's a typical mid-twenties asshole. He's got an income, a beautiful girlfriend, and he can't figure out why he's not happy. All he thinks with is his dick." I'd only met the guy once at a backyard barbecue and had an instant dislike for him. Rita was better off without him.

"He's not always like that," she said becoming defensive.

"Of course not," I said, backing off from my disgust. "No one is ever all one thing or another. But there is a development cycle for young men that gets in the way of knowing what they are looking for. Their lower animal functions rule over all the higher level reasoning."

"What do you mean?"

I opened the refrigerator and took out two grapefruits. I set them on the counter.

"What do you see?" I asked.

"I see two grapefruits," Rita responded.

"Exactly. Now if we brought Alex in here, what do you think he would see?"

"He'd have to see two grapefruits, wouldn't he?"

"He would," I answered. "He'd see two grapefruits and he'd get a hard-on." She laughed. It was good to see a break in the teary demeanor.

"Now," I said, deciding to continue the lesson. "Do grapefruits turn him on?" I only waited a couple beats before I continued. "No. It's a response to archetypal stimuli that he can't help. A guy like Alex will get a hard-on while he's shaving if his cock happens to bump against the bathroom sink."

"I've seen that happen," Rita said. Then she blushed crimson. "I thought it was because I was there." I looked at her with a real feeling of tenderness. Males were all sluts—especially young males. It was a hard lesson that every young woman should learn, even though it isn't pleasant. But how much happier they would be if they recognized the difference between synaptic response and real feeling.

"Sweetheart," I said, reaching up to stoke her cheek gently, "you are capable of turning on any man you desire. It's when a man responds to your desire that you connect; not when he responds to your shape. You just need to learn to recognize what you want and not assume that just being there is enough to get it."

"Do I turn *you* on?" she asked softly. Great. Now I was on the spot. I didn't want to offend her, but I had to be honest with her.

"Rita, it takes more than being in the presence of a beautiful woman to turn me on," I said. "When you want to turn me on, you will."

She looked at me and held my eyes with hers. I was afraid I'd gone to far, but she smiled shyly at me.

"I'd better get going before the neighbors start talking," she said, slipping off the bar stool. "Thank you for the tea and sympathy, Doc." She stood on tip-toe and kissed my cheek with a lingering tenderness, then turned toward the door. "Mind if I stop in to talk again some time?"

"Any time," I responded. Then she was gone.

———❊———

I'M NOT SEXUALLY deprived. I'd just never found the right combination of sex, love, and interest it took to become committed. Most of what I told Rita was just blowing smoke up her ass—which I'd dearly love to do. It was a week before I saw her again. I let her play an active role in my fantasies during that time, but I had a lot of work to do. I had open houses and showings.

I also managed to squeeze in a portrait sitting with a wealthy and good-looking woman named Sheila. I earned a living selling real estate. I spent my off hours painting in my studio. Sheila had heard I was discreet and would give her exactly what she wanted. I couldn't help but wonder what she'd heard. She wanted 'a sexy portrait' to give to her husband for their tenth anniversary. We finally agreed on a time and she came to my basement studio for a posing session.

After several sketches in different poses, she gradually started to relax her grip on the drape I'd given her. Sessions always start that way. 'Just in my bra and panties,' they'd say. 'Artfully draped.' 'Like an old master.' If they'd studied old masters like I had, they'd be naked on a pedestal when we started. I didn't treat my models that way. Eventually, the drape had slipped until her right breast was fully exposed. She liked the sketches and we worked on the pose a bit until we had her with her head tilted slightly away with eyes glancing toward the distance and the drape restored, so her nipple barely peeked out. I snapped a digital photo of the pose as well as the sketch and promised I would have the painting available in two weeks. She looked over my shoulder at the easel and let the drape fall to the floor.

It wasn't unusual to have a model lose her inhibitions as we worked, and more than one had completely lost control. I wasn't above taking advantage of the situation when it happened. I watched her (and her breasts) as she examined the sketch. I could see exactly what she was seeing as she looked at the sketch. Her hand rose to her cheek and tried to trace the line of her jaw in the way I'd drawn it. She explored the sketch by tracing her own body. She let her hand trace the position of the drape in the drawing, gliding across her chest to lightly touch her nipple. It was delicately shaped, and the way it rose as she caressed it let me know that she had probably not breast-fed her two children. Nipples tend to lose some of their sensitivity after an infant has sucked them dry day and night. Hers were obviously sensitive. She gasped at her own touch. She stood rigidly there for a moment without moving.

"May I come back to sit for the actual painting?" she asked with a quaver in her voice. My nostrils flared. Doing an oil or acrylic painting is a much longer process than doing the preliminary sketches. That's why I snap digital photos of the pose so I can use it for reference as I paint from the sketch. Sitting and holding one position for two or three hours (with occasional breaks to relax the muscles) is much different than the ten to fifteen minutes it takes to sketch a pose. But frankly, I'd much rather be referring to her fleshly presence as I painted than to the photo.

I agreed and we set a time. I would lay in the background and base. I'd be ready to focus on her when she came back. She dressed in front of me instead of going behind the changing screen, putting on her lacy bra and nearly sheer blouse, then arranging her hair. She would spend the week between now and our next appointment developing a strategy to seduce me. It wasn't the first time. I would spend the week developing a strategy to let her.

# 2
# Flirting

RITA SHOWED UP at my door on Friday evening as I was watching television. I was surprised as I figured that on the first night of the weekend she would be out on a date. I suppose it was too soon after the break-up for that. But she had a lot of friends she could be with.

Personally, I disliked the bar scene and if I hadn't actually arranged a date to go out with on Friday night, I stayed home.

"Hi, Doc," she greeted me. "Are you busy tonight? Can we talk some more?"

"I said any time, Rita," I answered, letting her into the house. "Why aren't you out tonight?"

"Because I suck," she said flatly. "I'm apparently just no good at it."

"Believe me as a man, there is no such thing as a bad blowjob," I laughed. She laughed a little nervously and I switched off the TV. I had opened a bottle of wine and didn't bother to ask if she wanted any. I just poured us both a glass and we sat companionably on the sofa for a few minutes before she started in.

"I don't know what I'm doing," she said finally. "I tried flirting with a couple of guys at work this week and discovered I couldn't tell if they were interested in me or just responding to the archetypal stimuli, as you put it. They both hit on me and I discovered I wasn't interested in them that much."

"That's a good sign," I said. "You respond to archetypal stimuli as well. They just happen to be different than the ones a man responds to. If you can distinguish the difference between a moistening between your legs and a genuine interest in a guy, that's a step in the right direction." She squirmed on the couch a bit and adjusted her position.

"I've been thinking about what you said the other day," Rita said.

"Good," I answered. "I'm glad you are learning to…"

"Not about that part," she broke in. "Well, partially about that. But more what you said about if I wanted to turn you on, I could." I caught my breath. Subtlety is not a trait of the young. Either she was going to attempt to seduce me or she was going to ream me for being an old pervert. While I admit to the latter, I was counting on the former.

"I realized that I don't know how," she continued. "I guess I got used to the automatic response men have. 'Has tits. Must fuck.' The idea of deciding who I want to turn on and then doing it leaves me blank. Would you teach me… show me how to do it? I mean, how to turn you on?" There it was in the open.

"Do you want to turn me on?" I asked gently. This was going to take a lot of will-power to resist the rush.

"I want to learn how to turn you on," she answered. "And I'd much rather learn from you than randomly experiment with guys I don't even like. I like you. I'd like to turn you on." I poured us each another glass of wine and we sipped. I nodded.

"I told you I'd respond," I said. "I'm not going to back out now that you've expressed an interest. But if you want to learn how, you won't be able to just go up to a guy you're interested in and ask him to teach you. Let's start from the beginning. We'll set up a little play-acting to get started." I stood and moved to sit on a stool at the breakfast bar, still clearly in her line of sight. "Let's say you've seen me and you're interested. It looks like I might be interested, too. What do you do?"

"Well, I guess I start flirting," she answered.

"Don't tell me. Show me."

She looked over the back of the sofa at me. I glanced her direction and our eyes made contact. She shifted herself to make her breasts more prominent and made a little kissy noise in my direction. I laughed.

"What?" she demanded.

"I'm not a dog," I said. "I don't come when you make a kissy noise. I'm not saying that most guys won't, but it won't be what you want. It just tells me you're hot to trot and I happen to be alone and available. No connection. Flirting needs to build up tension."

"See. I told you I suck," she moaned.

"No, you just haven't had practice engaging. There's nothing wrong with the things you were doing. They just happen to be a little premature. First, try just holding eye contact for a while. See what comes of that. Think about the kinds of things you've seen in movies, or scenes you've fantasized about." I resumed my pose at the bar and glanced toward her. It was perfectly timed as she glanced in unison. She dropped her eyes slightly and then raised them to look directly into mine. A slow smile spread across her lips as we looked at each other. She seemed to glance away and then back at me. Then she winked. I winked back.

I was suspicious that I was being played. Those moves were smooth and well-practiced. I could feel a stirring already. She started to giggle.

"That feels so silly," she said.

"Why? You did extremely well."

"It was embarrassing," she confessed. "I couldn't keep a straight face. It was so…" She faltered as realization fell across her face. "…intimate," she breathed. I was relieved. It was coming spontaneously and I no longer felt like I was receiving a practiced performance.

"Finding a point of intimacy—even across a crowded room—is a key stage in seduction. It makes you co-conspirators. You are in it together now."

"I liked it," Rita sighed. "I felt something."

"So, follow it up," I answered. "What comes next? You've established a connection. I've acknowledged it. Where do we go from here?"

"I come and join you?" she asked.

"No," I answered. "You lure me to you. That makes it clear that I haven't misunderstood. Again, no summoning like a dog or patting the seat next to you like you want me to jump up. Think of a way to invite me without using words." She thought about it for a few moments and then resumed her position. I leaned against the bar and glanced back at her. Her eyes were there to meet mine and this time they held. The smile crept across her lips again and I seriously thought about kissing them.

She took a sip of her wine and looked into the glass as if considering. Then she tilted her head slightly, looked me in the eye, and raised her empty glass. One eyebrow came up in question and I smiled at her. I picked up the wine bottle and approached her.

"May I?" I asked, directing the bottle toward her glass. She held it out and smiled warmly at me.

"Thank you," she said. "Won't you join me?" Beautiful. I sat next to her, filled my own glass, and raised it to her.

"Cheers," we both said and then laughed.

We set our glasses down and I turned toward her to be met face on with her lips. She pressed them against my own, demanding entrance with her tongue. It was nice, but this wasn't going to teach her anything. Reluctantly, I broke away and pushed her back in her seat.

"What?" she asked. "Didn't you like it?"

"Oh yes," I said. "I liked it. And as well as we know each other, we could progress to sitting here making out like crazy. We know each other and we know why we're here. But if you did that to a guy you just met or knew only casually, he'd either be headed for the door or headed for your panties in a heartbeat. You want the tension to grow. You don't just want me to have a hard-on; you want me to ache for you."

"I'm sorry but after that little invitation game getting you over here, I was just feeling so horny I lost control."

"Nothing wrong with feeling horny. In fact, it's a good indication that what you are doing is working. If you are getting turned on, chances are I am, too." She took another sip of her wine and looked at me with puppy-dog eyes that begged to be taken and taught.

"So, what should I do?" she asked.

"Well, we'd be talking once we got to the table," I said, "just like we have been. Maybe we'd have to get acquainted a little."

"Like asking you what you do for a living?" she asked.

"No," I said. "Guys get nervous when a girl asks that kind of question. In real estate, we call it a qualifier. Can you afford the property you are lusting after? Otherwise I'm wasting my time. And believe me, unless he's an arrogant fool, no man will think he can afford you. That's why people developed the lame introductions they use like 'What sign are you?' It's a subject to talk about without being too personal. Unfortunately, it doesn't reveal anything about the person. You get no further than where you started. What you need are questions that get a good conversation rolling without sounding lame. I'll start this time."

We settled in facing each other on the sofa and she waited expectantly.

"That's a beautiful locket you're wearing," I said, looking at her neck. She reflexively lifted her chin a fraction so I could see it better. "May I?" I asked, extending my hand. She nodded her assent and I lifted the locket letting my finger rest against the base of her throat lightly as I examined the locket. "It must be from someone very special," I finished, laying the locket gently back against her throat and sliding my finger out from under it. She shuddered a little as I withdrew. This time, however, she took the hint and engaged.

"My daddy gave it to me on my 16th birthday," she said. "It had a picture of him and one of me in it when he gave it to me." She lifted the locket and popped it open. "He doesn't know I replaced my picture with my mom's. It's not like I wanted them to get back together or anything. I'd outgrown that. It's more like it's the two of them that made me, so I carry around a bit of each of them."

"They sound like wonderful people," I said truthfully. I'd met both of them over the years. "Looking at them, it's no wonder you are so beautiful." She reddened just a little and from this distance I could see that the flush extended down her throat and onto her chest.

"Do you have family you are close to?" she asked.

"Two older brothers who used to beat the tar out of me when I was a kid. My folks have been gone years," I said, surprising myself by talking about my family to her. "My brothers have their own families. I like being with the kids because I can spoil them and then give them back to their parents. It's a just reward for the way they treated me as a child." We laughed.

"I've always thought having kids would be fun," she said, "but raising them would be hell. I think I'll leave the breeding to my sister."

"There is something cool about being the favorite aunt or uncle," I said. "I've made it my mission to see that their kids get some culture in their lives. Do you like art?"

"Yeah. What's the old saying? I don't *know* art, but I know what I like. Do you know a lot about art?"

"A fair amount," I admitted. Most of my neighbors knew nothing about my alter ego the artist. Most just knew me as a real estate agent. "I studied art in college—still dabble in it a little."

"Really?" she asked. "I didn't know that. Do you paint?"

"Yes. Paint and draw. Sculpt a little. I like to get my hands in the clay and feel the shape and texture of the object." She reached for my hands and turned them over to examine carefully. Then she looked back in my eyes.

"Do artists see things differently than other people?"

"That's hard to say," I answered. "We've all seen cartoons of artists like Picasso seeing a much different version of the world than we see. I'm not sure it's that radical. They just interpret what they see differently. Remember the grapefruit?" She laughed and nodded. "Well, I see the same thing you do, but I think about it differently. And differently than Alex, too. I think in terms of light and color, texture and chiaroscuro. It's like seeing something from every angle at once."

"How do you see me?" she asked. I almost said, 'As two grapefruits.' I caught myself short. There was an innocence and shyness about the question that let me know she genuinely wanted to see herself through my eyes. Well, she had certainly found the right means of turning me on. I've fallen in love with every model I've ever drawn.

"Why don't I sketch you," I said.

13

3

# Drawing Rita

"HERE? NOW?" SHE asked, startled. I'd just suggested that I sketch her and she looked around to see if I had a pencil and paper at hand. "On a napkin?"

"I'll do it with words. There are a lot of different media for art."

"Okay," she said. "How do you want me to pose?" She giggled a little, thinking she was making a joke.

"First, I'll just spend some time looking at you. I want to really see you," I said. "It's easy to get lost in your eyes, but I want to see all of you, from every angle." I heard a little catch in her breath at the implication, but she didn't move. True to what I was saying, I took the opportunity to drink her in. She was a mature woman of twenty-six years but I could still see the mischief and wicked sense of adventure she'd had as a school girl. She and her sister with a bunch of neighbor kids had once set up a water slide in my back yard because mine was the one with a slope to it. I remembered them in their bathing suits, splashing down the sheet of plastic. It wasn't difficult to think of the difference between the slight bumps that filled out their swimsuits then and the incredible breasts that filled out her blouse now.

I reached out and touched her hair, pulled back in a ponytail, hanging down over one shoulder. When I grazed her cheek, she involuntarily leaned in toward my fingers.

"I want to know the shape of your hairline and the texture of your hair. I look deeply at the softness of your skin and imagine what it

14

would feel like under my fingers' caress. I look at the shape of your face, the elegance of your neck. I want to know the breadth of your shoulders. I pause for a moment just to watch your breasts rise and fall with your breathing. I guide your face with my fingers so your eyes can look just over my left shoulder and I tilt your head slightly to emphasize your jawline.

"My first sketch is quick and near life-size on a sheet of newsprint, drawn with soft charcoal. I capture the centerline of your face and position of your eyes. I draw in the tip of your nose and the simplest rendition of your lips, letting the charcoal slide to the side to get more fullness in just one line." Rita's eyes fluttered as I traced the centerline of her face with my forefinger from the hairline to the tip of her chin. When I traced the shape of her lips with my finger, they trembled and parted slightly.

I continued, tracing the edge contour of her ear and hair and let my finger trail down her right shoulder and upper arm. Then, as if I were drawing on paper, I lightly grazed the depression where her throat met her collarbone and surprised her as I used a finger on each hand to trace from her collarbone, following the line of her blouse to the cleft between her breasts. Her eyes popped open wider, but she didn't shift her pose.

"With a rough sketch having shown me how you are put together, I switch to a smaller pad and a 4B pencil," I continued. "I adjust your pose slightly, tilting your head so I see the other ear and you are looking over my right shoulder. I lift your chin slightly and tease a soft smile from your lips." She nearly sucked my finger into her mouth as I stroked the corner of her mouth to get a little smile from her. I wondered if that was how da Vinci got the Mona Lisa's smile. She gasped and nearly collapsed when I continued.

"I loosen the top button of your blouse and slide the collar further over your right shoulder, moving the strap with it so it will not be in my composition. I'm ready to look at the play of light and shadows on your skin without lines. This time, I start with the shape of your eyes in the lamplight, smudging the tone to where I want it and deepening your sparkling eyes. I lay my pencil flat on the paper and, after lightly shading the lowlight of your cheek, I use my thumb to spread the graphite up toward the high point of your cheekbone, capturing it without a line between the inset of your eye and your cheek."

I was thoroughly enjoying the feel of her skin as I softly stroked her face and from the rate of her breathing, it was apparent she was enjoying it, too. She'd been caught in the mesmerizing narration of her body.

"I note how the shadow on your right defines the highlight of your nose and extends into your upper lip, receding in the depths of the corner of your mouth. Your chin doesn't define the end of your face, but rather the shadow of your neck reveals the shape of your chin. I find where the shadow stretches from your earlobe down beneath your jaw and smooth the tone to give shape to your throat, ending in the depths of the hollow at your collarbone." Rita was breathing notably faster and more shallowly as my fingers traced each part of her face and worked down her neck as I drew her in my mind. Had she been ticklish, the touch would have been torture, but she was merely sensitive and a deep flush had begun to slip from her face down her throat and over her breasts. I continued by tracing her collarbone out from the neck to the right shoulder where I had pushed her blouse and saw her eyes close as she absorbed my touch.

"Now I am ready to find a pose for my detailed sketch. I loosen the last buttons of your blouse so it falls away from your shoulder and down your arm. I slip your arm out of the sleeve and the strap of your bra so nothing interrupts the smooth flow of the line of your shoulder and arm. The arm is defined on the inside by your breast pressed against it. I turn you so you are nearly facing away from me and ask you to undo your ponytail." Rita glanced at me to confirm that I actually wanted her to do this herself and when I nodded, she reached up to loosen the knot and let her hair fall free. Before she could lower her arm, I held it gently in the position with her hand in her hair.

"I ask you to loosen your ponytail, not because I can't do it, but because I want to see the line on the underside of your arm," I said as I traced the line down along her smoothly shaved underarm and let my fingers part as they traced both the line of her back and her breast at the same time. A tiny mewling sound escaped her lips as my fingers trailed across her right breast. She was so used to my hands on her body now that she didn't flinch when I found the front clasp of her bra. I flicked it open and it fell to her side.

"The shadows here are tricky," I continued my narration as my hands gently stroked from her armpit down along the side of her beautifully exposed breast. Her eyes were once again closed, so she could not see how intently I feasted on the sight of her breast and the tiny pink nipple that in spite of its petite size seemed to stretch the skin taut as a drumhead. "I must be careful to capture the light and shadow as the hollow of your underarm stretches to meet the rise of your breast. The black and gray of the graphite seem so inadequate to capture the deep flush in your skin and the subtle darkening of your nearly transparent nipple sitting high on the proud mound of your breast. I need to capture in the shading the firmness and the softness, carefully blending the shadow into the crease beneath your breast so there is no plasticity in the rendering. I take great care to find the right shape and size of your nipple with the graphite clinging to my thumb."

The funny thing is that as I stroked her nipple with my thumb, my fingers applying light pressure beneath the breast, I could really see what it would look like on paper when I had drawn it. And I definitely would draw her. For her part, Rita was moaning aloud now, ready to collapse, but firmly holding herself in the pose I had created for her. I wanted to fall on that heaving breast and take the nipple between my lips, but that wasn't necessary to achieve what I desperately wanted now. I stuck with the drawing and extended my domain. The left side of Rita's blouse and bra still clung to her left breast, so I gently slid my palm across from her right, lifting the fabric up and away from her exquisite tit. She shrugged her shoulder slightly and the fabric slid down her arm and off her wrist. She was fully exposed now and her eyes watched me, even though she had not moved her right arm from the pose. God! If only all my models were so disciplined and compliant! In some sessions I found myself getting up every few minutes to correct the pose back to where I wanted it. Their antsy fidgeting destroyed the continuity of my drawing.

"Your breasts are twins but with such subtle individuality that only one intimately familiar with them could tell the difference. The right is flawless—translucent skin drawn tightly over a soft and pliable layer, perfectly shaped and crowned by a pink nipple, tinged with a wash of sienna. It deepens in color when you blush." As if called by my mention of it, the blush once again spread across her cheeks and chest. I softly caressed the contour of her breast to emphasize my point. "The left is equally flawless—the nipple fractionally darker in color and pointing slightly as if to call attention to her sister. A tiny dark dot on the breast just to the outside of the nipple cries out to be kissed, drawing attention back to the left." This time I permitted myself to lean forward and brush the tiny mole without sucking on the ripe little nipple. Rita breathed a long whispered, 'Ohhhhh.'

"I trace the contours of each breast, flowing down into the valley between," I continued. I let my fingers bunch around each nipple and as softly as water trickling down, I let them expand and slide down into her cleavage. This raised tiny bumps all across both breasts and up onto her shoulders. "From here, I continue my downward journey, parting the shadow like the waters of the sea until my pencil rests and deepens the shadow of your navel. This barely visible depth is the center of a field of white skin that continues to the sides until lost in the shadow of the background and plunges into unfathomed depths below."

At this point I dragged my fingers southward from her navel, over her slightly rounded stomach. As they progressed, her stomach muscles tightened—sucking the flesh inward—partly in response to my touch and partly, perhaps, in subconscious effort to give me easier access beneath the loosened waistband of her skirt. I slid my hand on down, keeping contact with her skin as her breathing quickened and began to come in gasps until I felt the soft brush of her hair and the very top of her slit. This at last was too much for my lovely Rita. Her upheld arm collapsed around my neck and she drew me to her in a passionate kiss from which she gasped, "Oh, Doc!"

I looked into her eyes as I held one arm around her naked shoulders and one hand still just deep enough below her panties to feel the moisture that was rapidly spreading. She crushed her lips to mine once more and thrust her tongue between my lips. Still, I teased and nipped the end of her tongue, pulling back far enough that she could not follow; then, with just the tip of my tongue moistening her lips before they parted again, we kissed deeply. When we parted from that embrace, she let her hand trail down the front of my shirt, unfastening the buttons in a near mimic of the slow dance I had used over her blouse. When the shirt was unbuttoned, she let her hand slip lower, where it glided over my very stiff cock.

"Have I turned you on, Doc?" she asked plaintively.

"Oh, my lovely Rita, you certainly have."

"Good," she answered, "because I so want to make love to you."

You might think there would be a maddened rush at this point, but Rita had been so captured by the slow and delicate maneuvers of my artistic description that she wanted to duplicate them herself. This she did, however, with more direct intent as she traced the line of my jaw with her tongue and massaged my chest with her hands. She slid down my body, finding first my right nipple and then my left with her tongue as her hands busied themselves with my belt and fly. She pushed my trousers down and I found the zipper for her skirt and slid it and the tiny lace panties she wore over her hips and down her legs. She rubbed my cock between her breasts and then slid up, pushing me back on the sofa as she moved over me. There were no more words spoken as she slid her pussy lips over my cock, but when she slid me inside her we both gasped and clutched each other tightly.

I've long prided myself on my stamina, but our foreplay had gotten me so turned on that I was afraid I would not last long enough to stroke a single time. I needn't have worried about it, however. We lay there relishing the feeling of being joined so deeply. Without moving or touching further, I felt Rita contract on my cock and cry out, then raise herself up and slam down, crying out again. Her vaginal convulsions were so strong in her orgasm that I stood no chance of withholding my own orgasm. In spite of my teeming fantasy with the rich model I had sketched earlier in the week, it had been some time since I'd actually taken care of the building tension in my balls and I exploded in Rita with a ferocity I'd seldom experienced before. Just as things began to settle from our mutual satisfaction, Rita would shift and convulse in an aftershock, eliciting one more spurt from my cock.

At last we lay, exhausted in each other's arms, my softening but still adequate cock lodged deep in her pussy. The perfect globes of her breasts were smashed against my chest, our nipples kissing each other. She lifted her face to me and I drank deeply of her kisses, our lips and tongues unwilling to leave each other.

We awoke in much the same position as we had fallen asleep, though only the tip of my cock still remained in contact with her labia. She looked into my eyes with a look that brought a stirring back to my member.

"Doc," she said softly. "Will you teach me everything? Please?"

"Yes," I said kissing her nose and eyelids. "Yes, my dear, everything."

4

# Painting Sheila

WHEN I AWOKE in the morning, Rita was gone.

Well, strictly speaking, it was barely morning. I lay in bed several minutes reliving every sensuous moment of the previous night, trying to convince myself it had not been an elaborate fantasy I put over on myself. When I realized what time it was, though, I jolted out of bed and dashed to the bathroom for a shower and shave. Saturday is a busy day in the real estate industry and I had an open house scheduled at one of my listings in less than an hour.

In the bathroom, my mirror had been decorated with lipstick. A curly border had been drawn around a series of XOXOXO and a perfect lipstick imprint of Rita's lips. It seemed there were no hard feelings. She must have had to work this morning, too. Or else she wanted to get across the drive and into her own house before daylight. I got dressed and made it to my open house with minutes to spare, then sat and waited for four hours while a sparse trickle of visitors came, showing no interest in the house whatsoever. Some days are like that. I entertained myself between visitors by sketching small details I could remember from the night before. I discovered Rita could turn me on without even being in the same room.

I didn't see Rita at all for the rest of the weekend. She had taken off Saturday morning with a bunch of girlfriends for a girls' weekend at a local spa. She called Saturday night and said she'd see me sometime the next week.

21

MONDAYS ARE DEAD in the real estate industry unless you happen to have landed a fish during a weekend open house. I considered Monday my weekend. Tuesday morning, I would have to deal with brokers' open houses and a new homes tour, but Mondays, I reserved to paint. The inestimable Sheila Monroe, my wealthy client, called and asked if she could sit for her painting that afternoon. I'd laid in the background and washes, and was ready to start on the detail work. I agreed and Sheila arrived about noon.

She didn't bother to step behind the privacy screen I keep in the studio for changing, but made sure she had my eye first and began simply taking her clothes off in front of me. This was a portrait that showed down almost to her draped waist, but she took off considerably more clothing than was strictly required. She stood in a lacy transparent thong and waited for me to position her on the couch in the pose I'd recorded. I spread a blanket on the chaise I was using to pose her on and she settled into position. I looked at the position in the photo and made several small adjustments to her posture and position, letting my hand rest gently on her shoulder or back as she got comfortable.

I'd warned her that sitting for a painting was not like sitting for a sketch. The process is much slower and therefore, the pose must be held much longer. I usually work for forty-five minutes and then take a break for fifteen so the model has time to get the blood circulating through her limbs again. After the first session, Sheila was stiff and tired of the same pose, but she dropped her drape and pranced around the studio—loosening up, she said—in just her thong. She leaned over my shoulder to look at the progress on the painting, pressing up against me.

Sheila is in her mid-thirties and has two children, but in true trophy wife fashion, she's taken immaculate care of her body. She chatted as we worked through the next session about her busy schedule of getting the children up and off to school and meeting friends at the tennis club to play and enjoy the spa. She might have a massage scheduled—with Enrico, her favorite therapist—or just have lunch and a glass of wine.

At least three times a week, she met with a personal trainer, who had obviously been doing a great job. She is about five-five and her body is lean and trim. Almost too lean for my tastes as, like most artists, I like to see curves in a woman. Nonetheless, there is nothing unpleasant about looking at her.

In the third and final forty-five-minute session, there was something slightly different about her pose. Checking the digital photo, I didn't see what it was at first. A slight movement after I'd started painting, however, drew my attention downward. Sometime during her last break, she'd lost the thong and the drape had been pulled up far enough to expose a clear view of her pussy. I tried to keep my focus on the curve of her breast and the nipple peeking from behind the drape, but I noticed the hand that was not in the picture had slipped beneath the sheet and was slowly stroking her cleanly shaved pussy.

I had a new admiration for Sheila. In fact, I was beginning to think I might call her to model for me professionally sometime. She was holding her upper body perfectly still in the pose we'd agreed on, even while fingering her clit. That takes some concentration and I was losing mine. I managed to complete the curves I was working on and then said I thought we'd done enough for today.

"Oh, Doc," she said as she moved and adjusted the sheet again, making sure my view was unobstructed. "Would you mind doing just a couple more sketches of me that are full-body and not just upper?" She was lying naked in front of me, so I had no difficulty agreeing.

I brought my sketchbook and a bit of charcoal and sat my stool much closer than I had for the portrait. She moved herself into a reclining pose and positioned the drape so she was full exposed. I quickly lay in a charcoal sketch and captured the bare slit she was showing with her fingers poised just over it. When I'd finished the sketch, she shifted positions and the drape fell away entirely with no pretense about using it for modesty. She arched herself backward, spreading her legs slightly and I tore through another rapid sketch. I had a feeling this was less about me sketching and more about her posing.

"What do you think of my ass?" she asked, getting on her hands and knees for the next pose. She pointed it pretty directly at me and I could see her labia open, exposing her channel and clit. "I'd like you to do one that is just a close-up of my derriere."

"It's a lovely ass, Sheila," I said as I positioned my stool close enough to smell her and see the fine details of her ass and pussy. Between the posing and her earlier fingering, moisture glistened around her pussy lips. I sketched each little pucker as I saw it and, in a few minutes, I had a likeness that only her husband would recognize. Or perhaps her masseur.

She got up from the chaise and looked at the sketches.

"Is that really what I look like from that angle?" she asked.

"Yes," I said. "It's really quite beautiful."

"No wonder George likes it so much!" she exclaimed. I had to assume George was her husband, but perhaps it was her personal trainer. She sat on my lap and pulled the sketchbook from my hands. "You could almost reach out and touch it."

"From where I am right now, I could," I laughed. It was very pleasant to have this woman sitting and wiggling on my lap the way she was. I was beginning to show signs of my arousal.

"Why don't you?" she whispered in my ear. She dropped the sketchbook on the floor and wrapped her arms around me, coming in for a wet, sloppy kiss.

When I pay a model to sit for me, we work hard and maintain a good professional distance. I never touch a model without permission and then only guide her (or him) to the pose I specifically want. That isn't to say I've never enjoyed other entertainment with a model after we'd closed up the studio, but I keep work and pleasure strictly separate when money is changing hands.

In this case, however, the woman was paying me for painting her and was not a professional model. I had no compunction about filling my hands with her ass and burying my face in her tits. And there was no doubt that Sheila was not only willing, but expected no less.

Fucking Sheila was a far cry from making love to Rita. I am by nature a more languorous lover, but Sheila was a woman on a mission and I contented myself with being the fulfillment of her fantasy—and enjoying the experience as she pulled at my clothing until I was fully naked as well. Though I was swelling with anticipation, it takes some slight direct stimulation before I'm fully ready to consummate a relationship. Noting this, Sheila fell to the task with vigor, teasing my cock fully upright with her tongue and lips. Though she applied herself diligently, I was loath to release my load between her lips as I'd seen a far more appealing target.

I lifted her to her feet and guided her back to the chaise, where I set forth to return the oral pleasures to her. My experience is not as broad as you might expect an artist's to be. I have had an adequate supply of lovers over the years, but I'm not the type to need sex on a daily or hourly basis. Experience has shown me a few things, however. It is not unusual for professional models to shave their privates for the sake of art. When I sketch a woman, having a great bush of hair between her legs has approximately the same effect as airbrushing the region out of existence. When I was in school, student models would often arrive who shaved nothing. It was a part of the "back to nature" movement from which we were able to draw so many of our models. My first experience with an atelier model, however, changed the way I looked at the female form—from an artistic perspective, of course.

From a purely sexual perspective, a shaved pussy does no more to stimulate me than a hairy one. I have discovered, however, a woman who shaved for other than professional reasons, did so with intent. The intent was to attract oral attention to the area. When I buried my face between Sheila's legs, I found she was as smoothly bare as the proverbial baby's bottom. When I applied my tongue to the slippery slit, the response was… shall we say, noisy. She was verbal beyond words, helping to spread her labia to give me better access as she screamed over and over such lovely endearments as, "Yes! Fuck yes!" and, "Oh oh oh oh."

Having such an enthusiastic recipient for oral sex made me much happier to give it. She tasted sweet and slightly salty from her juices. I explored every juicy fold of her labia with the tip of my tongue, thrusting it as deeply into her pussy as I could before dragging it up, out, and over her clit to more shuddering cries. As I worked on her clit with my tongue, I explored the region with my fingers as well. She had flooded the area with so much slippery juice that it ran between her legs and down her ass. I used my thumb in her pussy, pumping in and out as I flattened my tongue against her clit and wiggled it back and forth. My middle finger, I placed against her back door and began gently to apply pressure. This led to a new crescendo in her vocalese and a long string of "Fuckfuckfuckfuckfuckfuck," deteriorating into a long loud wordless wail. I did not let up until she clamped her legs shut on my ears, yelling, "Stopstopstop. I can't take anymore. Please, stop!"

Whenever a woman tells me to stop, I do—whether it is at the beginning or at the end or any point between. The grip she had on my head with her thighs prevented me from actually withdrawing, so I released her clit from my tongue and gently kissed her pussy, in which my thumb was still buried. My finger as well, I did not withdraw from her anus. On both, I could feel the continued pulsing as she came down from her orgasms. Gradually, the pressure on my ears relaxed and I was able to raise my head slightly to look at her. She was looking down at me with a mixture of satisfaction and curiosity, as though she were trying to figure out who I was and how I got my head between her legs.

"Mmm. That was just what I needed," she said, smiling. Then she heaved a bit of a sigh. "I suppose you want to fuck me since you wouldn't come in my mouth," she continued. She rolled over, pulling my fingers from her. On her knees with her ass in the air, she was in much the same pose as I'd sketched. "Use whichever hole you want, but be quick about it. I need to get home and shower before George does."

I was being given my choice of fucking her pussy or her ass from behind, but somehow the joy had gone out of it. I may have been hard, but I couldn't see myself fucking an uninvolved ass or pussy.

"Not necessary, Sheila," I heard myself saying as I patted her ass. I turned away to pick up my clothes. "I'm just happy you're satisfied." She looked at me a little strangely, as if I weren't quite human.

"Your loss," she said, gathering her clothes and stepping behind the privacy screen. "You should have come while I was blowing you." I had to chuckle at that while I stuffed my cock back into my trousers and felt it reluctantly let go of its stiffness. After I assured Sheila the painting would be done in a week, she asked for the three new sketches I'd done and I gladly gave them to her. She left, promising she'd be back for another sitting 'if I needed her.' I highly doubted that. She'd gotten what she wanted. The act of sitting for her portrait had made her horny and she had built up her own fantasies about how to seduce me. She wanted no doubt left in my mind that this was a one-time opportunity and it would never occur again.

I cleaned up the studio and gathered up the towels and drape to be laundered. I checked behind the screen to be sure nothing had been left and, somewhat to my surprise, found five one-hundred-dollar bills on the changing table.

What can you do? I had to laugh and decided to find a charity to give my ill-got gains to.

# 5
# Like a Firehose

I CAME AWAKE SLOWLY, finally realizing the ringing I was hearing was not my alarm clock, but the doorbell. It was nearly one o'clock Friday morning. I jumped out of bed, into my slippers and robe, and rushed to the door, thinking there might be an emergency of some sort. Perhaps someone had seen smoke coming from my house!

I opened the door and saw my lovely Rita leaning against the doorjamb.

"Hi, Doc!" she exclaimed cheerfully. She'd been drinking. I couldn't tell how much, but she had that pleasantly buzzed look about her and was grinning happily at me. "Aren't you going to invite me in?"

"Sure," I said. "I did say any time." As soon as I closed the door behind her, she turned and kissed me deeply.

"Sorry I haven't been over sooner," she said. "I wanted to, but things just weren't working out the way I planned."

"You had a plan?" I asked. Cobwebs were still clearing from my head. If she arrived to make love, I'd just lead her back to my bed.

"Just to get back here as soon as I could," she said. "There was the stupid girls' spa weekend, then work, and I got my period. I just didn't feel like I could come over here like that." I would have to disabuse her of that inhibition eventually. "So, I was out with the girls tonight for our Thursday night whine and dine and I got to missing you terribly and I wanted to know more and I was feeling… well, lustful. And there was this discussion."

While she was rattling on, she'd dropped her purse and coat on the floor and stepped out of her shoes. I wasn't directing, but she was nudging me in the direction of my bedroom. I wasn't inclined to resist.

"What kind of discussion?" I asked.

"In a minute," she said. "First I gotta pee." She ducked into the master bath and closed the door. Left waiting, I fluffed a pillow so I could sit up in bed and slid back beneath the covers. It took her a while and, in spite of myself, I was nodding off when the bathroom door opened. Rita stood there, framed in the light, completely naked. "You don't mind that I got more comfortable, do you?" I took in the vision of loveliness before me and pinched myself to be sure I was awake.

She'd taken her hair down out of its usual ponytail and it fell softly around her shoulders. The light filtering through the light brown locks was like an aura around her face. Her shoulders rose and fell with her breathing and that drew my attention to her pert breasts. I couldn't help but make a mental note about how much plumper they were than the voraciously demanding Sheila. Despite their fullness, the nipples were tiny dots in the middle of barely perceptible areolae. At her height of just over five feet, the thick bush of her pussy was just a bit above the edge of the bed where she stood posing for me.

As if on cue, she pirouetted slowly to her left until she came to a stop with her back to me. Her shoulders gently sloped from the base of her neck where her hair parted to either side. A small beauty spot was just below her right shoulder blade, and much to my surprise, there was a tiny butterfly tramp-stamp tattooed at the base of her spine. I admit that in the low light of our love-making, that had escaped notice. It drew my attention to her tiny waist and beautifully round buttocks with the tantalizing crack between. She continued her pirouette and I noticed as she came into profile how proudly her breasts rode on her chest. When she was facing me again, she smiled like the proverbial cat that ate the canary.

"I know you like to just look first," she giggled. "See? I did learn something." We both laughed at that. She put her hands on the foot of the bed and crawled up on it, stalking toward me until our lips could meet.

"What a delightful way to wake up in the middle of the night," I said as our lips parted. "Come, get under the covers with me."

"Nope," she said, sitting back abruptly. She sat cross-legged facing me and I could see her pussy lips part her bush as the glistening sheen of moisture between her legs caught the lamplight. "I wanna talk."

"O-kay," I said, drawing out the word as I enjoyed the view. "What would you like to talk about?"

"What's the big deal with blowjobs?" she asked.

"What?" She had shifted gears again and I was catching up. Having all my attention on her pussy was probably contributing to my slowness.

"Well," Rita began, "the girls were discussing this over drinks tonight. The discussion turned to men and that led to sex and that led to blowjobs. Pamela said she'd rather give a guy a blowjob than have sex with him. Carmine said she had such a bad gag reflex she couldn't get a cock past her lips without throwing up. And Jan said blowjobs were just a normal part of having sex and you had to do them if you ever wanted to get any satisfaction for yourself. We don't exactly take turns when we're talking, you know, so everybody had more to say on the subject and it was all pretty interesting. Eventually, they noticed I hadn't said anything and they all started to stare at me and thought I had some big secret I wasn't telling them. I finally blurted out that according to Alex, I couldn't suck water from a firehose. At first, they thought I was kidding and then they started to get furious. They said it was his fault if he didn't enjoy putting his dick in my mouth and I should go find someone who appreciated me. I thought, I know someone who appreciates me. So, what was I doing sitting around moaning with these bitches when I could be in his arms and he'd tell me what the big deal was and then I'd be able to suck water from a firehose?"

I swear, she paused for the first breath she'd taken since she started. Once she got wound up, it was just a flood of confusion and emotion pouring out of her. "So, what's the big deal with blowjobs?" she asked again.

I laughed gently. "I assume you mean other than they feel great and fuel fantasies," I said. She punched my leg softly.

"I mean it," she said. "I want the primal archetype men respond to. You seem to know one for everything."

"Ah." I could see already she wanted to be told she was good at oral sex, but there had to be a story to go along with the urge. So, I made one up. "Every guy wants to believe his girl could have sex with four or five guys at once," I began.

"Alex wants me to have sex with a basketball team?" she exclaimed, raising her eyebrows.

"No, no. Some guys get off on that kind of thing, but we're talking about the archetype, not some aberration," I said. "No, he just wants to believe that you could have sex with four or five guys at once."

"And exactly how would I do that?" she asked. "It's ridiculous."

"Hmm. You certainly know basic sex with cock in pussy," I answered slowly. She nodded. "And you at least know there is oral with cock in mouth. Then there is cock in hand, cock in ass, and cock between the breasts. That's five and doesn't count having two hands available. See? Up to six by that count."

"All at once? I'd never keep them straight!"

"They'd stay straight, believe me." We laughed together at that and I decided to make up as much of a story as I could. "Like I said, he doesn't actually want you to do it, just to think that you could do it. And that you'd satisfy all six of them equally."

"But why?" she asked, plaintively. I was on a roll, so why stop now.

"We live in a society that is polarized between pornography and religion," I said. "On one side, you have Hollywood—and I use the term loosely—and on the other side, you have the church. I use that term loosely as well. One is telling you sex is good, sex sells, sex with a lot of people is even better, sex with people watching is best of all. On the other side, sex is part of an inviolable institution and is limited to a partnership between just two people for all eternity. The tension builds up inside. On one hand, a guy wants to have sex with every woman he sees. On the other hand, he wants to mate for life with the one woman who will be all he ever needs."

"Come on," Rita said. "No guy wants to have sex with every woman he sees."

"There may be some who escape his notice at first," I answered. "And some are dismissed with scarcely a thought. But once a woman is in a man's focus his first thought is about whether she would be a good fuck. He might dismiss the notion, but every woman he meets gets evaluated first based on her potential as a sex partner. Now the thing is that a guy who's serious enough to actually have sex with her is going to have this voice in his ear hounding him that this could be the last person he ever has sex with. She could be the one he marries. This might be the only pussy he ever penetrates from now on."

"Guys don't have that much brainpower to think all that while they're fucking," Rita said dismissively.

"True," I said. "I'm just talking through what goes into the desire. See, if a guy figures you could have sex with four or five guys all at once, then having sex with you could be like having sex with four or five different women. Having a different woman for every day of the week no longer feels like the trap of monogamy. He might get through it after all."

She looked at me, puzzled for a moment. Then, sure she had a perfect counter-argument, she launched in. "Porn videos always show every way of having sex in every video. First you give a hand-job, then a blowjob, then he fucks you missionary, then he fucks you doggy or in the ass, and finally he comes on your face or your tits. That's the archetype that men see and want."

"But," I said, "porn is made for the pleasure of the viewers, not of the actors. They have fifteen, maybe twenty minutes of film time to get someone they don't know and will never meet up and off. They don't know what will turn on each viewer most, so they have to throw in a bit of everything. The guy watching the movie might come during the blowjob, the butt-fuck, or the come-shot. The only sure thing is that he'll come. That's why he bought the movie. The guy and gal in the movie have to act as though everything is giving them pleasure and, eventually, at least the guy has to come so success can be filmed. The girl can fake it and the camera won't know the difference. Most guys can't tell the difference for that matter."

She considered what I said while she sat cross-legged on the bed. It was getting close to what she really wanted and, as ridiculous as what I'd said was, just sitting here talking about sex had gotten her aroused, as the damp spot on the bedspread beneath her pussy attested.

"Five ways," she said and looked up at me a little bashfully. "Teach me to suck water from a firehose, Doc," she said simply. With those words, I felt a stirring in my groin. This was going to be a very good night—or morning.

⁓ ❧ ⁓

"Ungh!" I croaked out. My flaccid penis had just been vacuumed into my lovely Rita's mouth with such force, I thought the balls would follow. I gently pulled her back, finally wedging a finger between her lips and my prick to break the suction seal. "Sweetheart. Rita. Wait." She looked up at me with such a crease between her eyes, I thought she was going to break down and cry.

"It's true!" she cried out. "You don't like it either! I can't suck worth shit." Tears were leaking out her eyes. I pulled her close to me and rocked her.

"You asked me to teach you, Rita, and I said I would. You want a very special kind of skill that is above and beyond simply sucking. Now, you can't go crying when I'm trying to teach you."

"Really? It's just a lesson? Okay." She looked at me expectantly. I couldn't help but chuckle.

"First, I'm not a kitchen appliance."

"Huh?" She was completely perplexed.

"You have to turn me on before you plug me in!"

33

"Oh. You mean we have to go through that whole flirting and seduction routine every time we do something sexy?" she asked.

"No, no, no. But usually, you can't just go for the goods unless we've already got started. And…" This was a difficult one. "I don't expect you to be a vacuum cleaner. That's a delicate instrument down there. The term 'suck' is a catchall phrase, not always a literal instruction. Just like you don't just blow because it's a blowjob. No amount of pure suction will pull the juice out of my balls."

"But they always say… I mean… What about sucking water through a firehose?" I really laughed this time. How did this poor girl with all her scientific education get to be twenty-six and still be this naïve? For that matter, how did the cheerleader get out of high school this uneducated?

"Rita, when was the first time you gave a guy a blowjob?"

"Umm. Well. It was Alex, actually. I just never could imagine doing it, but he kept asking and I thought my pussy just wasn't enough to satisfy him and I'd have to suck him, so I just did it. A couple of weeks ago. And then he said I was…"

"The idiot. You mean he just told you it was terrible without offering suggestions about how to improve?" She nodded. I revised my estimate of his mental age down to about thirteen. "Okay. Here's what we're going to do…"

⊰◈⊱

AFTER A FEW minutes' instruction, Rita stretched out beside me and began a lovely, gentle kiss. Whatever she lacked in fellatio experience, she certainly possessed in kissing. Her lips were soft and she used them to pluck at mine until I opened to her. Then her tongue began a dance so elaborate, mine could not keep up. It swept across my lips, moistening them. Before I could catch it, it disappeared back into her mouth, begging me to chase it. Her lips embraced mine and again her tongue darted in and out of my mouth so quickly I was caught with my tongue waving in the air as she pulled away. I growled as I pushed my mouth toward hers and suddenly it was all softness and yielding—accepting my tongue and stroking around it with her own.

"That kissing talent is what you need to bring to a blowjob," I whispered.

There is nothing like a kiss to put wood in my pecker and as she trailed her fingers down my chest and belly, I was eager to feel her touch it. She did, but so lightly that, like her tongue on my lips, it was there and gone. Her lips, in fact, were gone from mine as her tongue followed the trail of her fingers over my chin and down my throat, pausing to kiss my Adam's apple as it bounced when I swallowed. She detoured off to playfully kiss my right nipple, again swirling her tongue around to excite me so much, I almost missed feeling her fingers return up my leg to tickle my balls.

A quick kiss to my eyelids, nose, and lips, and Rita settled back to my left nipple, this time suckling more intently but not with vacuum cleaner strength. The light nip of her teeth on my nipple came at the exact moment her palm pressed against the tip of my cock to smear a copious amount of pre-come across the head and down. Oh yes, she had turned me on. And in the process gave me some indications of things she might like as well.

She did not simply slide down my body, but pivoted, so by the time she had kissed down my pubes—carefully avoiding contact with my cock—she had curled with her pussy within my reach. I was about to touch it when she arrested her kissing near my knee and lifted her right breast so that only the nipple came in contact with the slippery end of my cock. She used her hand to guide my cockhead around her nipple, smearing it with lubricant from my cock.

Sliding farther toward the head of the bed, she took the hand reaching for her pussy and placed it on her breast, guiding my thumb to smear the lubrication around her nipple. As I did, her mouth hovered near my cock and I felt her breath catching as it blew in little pants across my balls. Her tongue reached out again and took little licks across the base of my cock near the scrotum. She laved my erection with her tongue, bringing her hand up finally to guide my cock and steady it as she worshipped it with her mouth.

She looked up at me over the head of my cock with an eyebrow raised, seeking reassurance. Apparently, she found it in my blissful expression as I looked into her eyes. She returned to her ministrations.

The pre-come rubbed into her nipple was drying, so I dragged my hand along her wet snatch, picking up a fresh batch of lubricant to smear across the nipple again.

Following my earlier advice, she made love to my cock with her mouth as if she were kissing me and my cock had replaced my tongue. And oh! Could she kiss!

She raised herself up and moved over me, careful to not bring her pussy in range of my mouth. She'd made it clear that she did not want to be distracted by my tongue on her clit while she practiced orally pleasuring me. But giving me access to her wet folds and being close enough that I could both see and smell her arousal was proving pleasurable for both of us. I stroked from her ass to her clit just as she lowered her mouth over my cock. The moan it elicited hummed across my skin electrically. My cock jerked, and realizing the vocalism had an effect, she proceeded to hum as she let her soft lips stroke up and down.

There was a seal and some suction as she moved her mouth, but this time, it simply drew more blood into my prick, making it stiffer and more sensitive than ever. Her mouth was a soft and welcoming channel fucking my cock. She used her hand to follow her mouth up and down my shaft, spreading the slipperiness until it felt like my entire cock was working its way in and out of her mouth, though I knew she had not attempted to take me into her throat.

I was nearing my climax and whispered, "I'm near." I felt one of her hands slip into her folds with mine and as I exploded, she twitched with a gasp that nearly made her inhale my come. Instead, it spattered across her face, her lips, and her tongue as she continued long sensuous strokes up and down with both her mouth and her hand.

She may have swallowed some, but certainly most of my spend was on her face and in her hair with a good portion on my own belly.

My fingers, lodged in her pussy, were likewise drenched. She looked back up at me, flicking a drop of come from her eyelid. The sensuous smile and gentle squeeze she gave me brought another small spurt out onto her fingers.

"It is like a firehose," she said dreamily. Not letting go for a moment, she continued kissing my cock. She scooped what cum remained on her cheek off and smeared it across her nipple before drawing my hand back to that breast to massage the slippery mass as we rose toward pleasure again.

## 6
## Christening

I GRADUATED FROM COLLEGE with an MFA in Visual Arts and a real estate license. It was my father's fault.

He was always supportive of my art career but he was a realist as well. He didn't tell me I'd need "a real job" in order to survive.

"Few art careers get launched straight into success. You're good, Dimitri. But becoming known can be a long slow process. It's unlikely that in this society you'll find a patron to support you. You're going to need a way to earn a respectable living during the time before you're famous. You also need something that is independent and flexible so you aren't too exhausted to paint." His solution was real estate. He promised to pay for my schooling, all the way through the MBA, if I got my real estate license and had made at least one solid sale before I graduated.

It was brilliant. At age 25, I had banked enough commissions to buy a nice house in a good neighborhood. It even had room for my studio. When I moved in, I was the youngest homeowner in the community. The neighbors were friendly and I invited everyone to a party the day my furniture arrived.

The lower level family room was on the north side of the house and had terrific light for painting. The house was on the edge of the development with a wooded greenbelt behind it and the windows were high, so reasonably private. Of course, there were a few close calls when the neighborhood kids romped through my yard on their way to the woods and got curious but, to my knowledge, none ever got an eyeful of my models.

The surprise was, I actually liked selling real estate. Oh, I didn't love it like I loved painting, but as far as earning a living went, it wasn't bad. I had co-workers who loved to party, met a lot of interesting clients, and occasionally, I really helped someone on their life journey.

That was the case with Allison.

She'd become the trophy wife of a corporate executive when she was in her early twenties. When she was thirty-five, the bastard traded her in on a newer model. She'd convinced herself that she really loved the guy and not just his money, so the divorce was bitter. The financial settlement of half of everything he owned took a bit of the sting out of it. It turned out that he owned a lot more than she was aware of, but her attorney located assets the court awarded to her. And because he tried to conceal assets, the court also made him pay all the attorney fees and court costs. Still, it took a big bite out of her self-confidence.

"It's funny," she said as we were touring houses looking for a new place for her to live, "but I couldn't imagine anyone younger or prettier than me being willing to sell herself to that old bastard. I thought as long as I was careful to keep my looks up and always be willing to satisfy him, I'd have lifelong security. I know, I'm a poor little rich girl, but it still hurts." I sympathized and dug further into the kind of life she wanted now, so I could match her up with a new house.

I admit to my prejudices. When I first met her and heard the story, I compared her to Sheila Monroe. Here's another of those beautiful women who think that's all that matters and everyone should worship her because she's beautiful. As we worked for a few weeks on matching her up with a new house, I got a very different impression. Allison was smart and funny. She had a credible self-understanding and knew what people as prejudiced as me thought of her. Her attitude convinced me she wasn't as high maintenance as I expected. As she got more caught up in her search for the perfect home, she developed a sense of relief that she didn't need to maintain the pretenses she had adopted as a CEO's wife. She wanted a much simpler lifestyle.

I finally found the right house for her.

It was a beautiful house, but much smaller than I expected to sell her. It was on a large lot that was mostly wild with very little lawn to maintain. It was in a good neighborhood and had enough room to entertain but not so much she couldn't clean it herself in a pinch. The day she closed on the house, I was sad that I would no longer be seeing her. We'd been together touring and negotiating at least twice a week for over a month. She was very nice company.

"I can't believe it's mine!" she said as we left the escrow office. I lifted my hand to give her the keys and she did a little happy dance on the sidewalk. "Come over and help me celebrate," she said. "I just need to stop by Costco and pick up a few things on the way. Can you come by about six?"

"I'd love to celebrate with you," I said. "Why don't I bring a bottle of champagne?"

"I'll see you then!"

I had plenty of time to stop by a wine store and pick out a decent but not overpriced bottle of bubbly and some flowers. I didn't mind spending fifty bucks on a house-warming gift. I'd just made about $10,000 in commission on the house she bought. I was celebrating, too!

I stopped back home to check my messages. There was a very brief message from Rita saying tomorrow was the big night. She was going to try to seduce Alex back and try out her newly-learned skills. I sighed. We'd been 'rehearsing' this for a few weeks. Whenever a new question about the art of loving struck her, we'd end up in bed together. She was an enthusiastic pupil and I was going to miss her when she got back with Alex. I still thought it was a bad idea, but I couldn't really start competing with him. It just wouldn't be right.

That poor guy, I chuckled to myself. He didn't stand a chance against her powers of seduction.

I ARRIVED AT Allison's door with the champagne chilled and the flowers fresh.

The door was standing open and I raised my hand to knock when she flew out the door and almost knocked me over. I caught her as she stumbled into me and the flowers went flying. The champagne, I managed to keep a grip on.

"Oh my God! What a rush!" she laughed as she clung to me for balance. "Sorry! Are you okay?"

"Yes, I'm fine. Is everything all right?"

"Yes. I just have a few more things in the car. I was trying to get everything in before you got here. Go on in and I'll be right back."

I stooped to gather up the scattered flowers and glanced up to see Allison leaning into the backseat of her Audi. She'd changed clothes since her closing and was completely relaxed in a pair of gray yoga pants and a red crop top T-shirt. When she leaned over, the pants hugged her shapely ass. The bottom hem of the T-shirt dropped away from her body and I could see up to the lower curve of her left breast. From the distance, I couldn't make out detail, but it was obvious she definitely got comfortable before I dropped by.

I straightened up as she approached with a box of supplies apparently just purchased from Costco, and followed her into the house.

"Is there anything else I can get from the car?"

"No, this was the last of it. How about rolling this out in front of the fireplace and lighting the gas jets. Then you can open that champagne." She busied herself in the kitchen opening cupboards and pushing boxes into them, apparently at random. A couple of boxes she opened and began emptying onto the counter. I watched with one eye as I took the rug she pointed to, cut the cords, and rolled it out in front of the living room fireplace on top of the already thick plush carpeting.

Allison was a beautiful woman. If she had a mind to go out and conquer another rich executive, I had no doubt it would be easy for her. But during our conversations, she made it clear that she'd made her millions and she didn't need to sell her body to the richest exec she saw. She was tall—easily five-eight—with shoulder length blonde hair that showed about an inch of reddish brown at the roots. She'd said she was through with the bimbo look and would be her natural color soon.

She was well-endowed physically as well as financially. There was a gentle sway that confirmed my opinion she had no bra beneath the T-shirt she wore. But while dressed in the epitome of casual wear, it also looked like her sweats had been tailored to show off her superb ass. I leaned against the breakfast bar and worked on the champagne cork as I watched her move. My thoughts weren't all that lascivious. I thought about how I'd paint her. She was Winged Victory, Aphrodite, and Rosie the Riveter all rolled into one. I thought I'd like to catch her before her hair finished growing out. If I could make it stand up, it would look like an angelic halo around her head. What a mass of contradictions.

Aside from the rug I'd just thrown on the floor and the champagne glasses she set on the counter, there was no furniture in the house. As we chatted, our voices echoed in the way that only an empty house can create.

"Isn't this great? I have my own place. No one can tell me to pick up my socks; no one can tell me what to wear; no one can dirty it up and expect me to clean it. No one except me."

"It sounds like a dream come true."

"You're a man. You wouldn't understand."

"I'm a man who has lived alone in my own space with no one to tell me when to come or go for the past fifteen years," I said.

"Okay. Maybe you would understand. But you're still a man." I poured the champagne and handed her a glass.

"So, are you swearing off all men then?" We clinked our glasses together.

"Here's to my new home," she said, downing the first glass of champagne in one long swallow and refilling her glass herself. "No, I'm not swearing off all men. I'm swearing off all relationships and entanglements." We took the bottle and our glasses and settled down on the new rug in front of the gas fireplace. I'm a coward. When I sense a woman ready to vent, I clam up. I sat there silently, waiting for her to continue and hoping I didn't become a stand-in target for all the people who had controlled her life. But she seemed to settle down immediately.

"I chose the life I lived. Jacob was good to me, but let's face it: he married me on the rebound after his first marriage went sour and I made the most of the opportunity. I convinced myself I loved him and sold my youth for a lifetime of security. I got it, even in divorce. With half his wealth, I'm not going to squander it or run to another sugar daddy. I don't need to live that way anymore."

We were sitting on opposite sides of the rug and she was now on her third glass of champagne as I drank from my first. She kept up with her impromptu lecture.

"Let's say I want to go to Hawaii for a week to go parasailing. I can just do it. If I want to sit in an expensive restaurant and eat a meal just to enjoy the food, I can do it without feeling I need to impress my husband's friends and associates." She set her glass down on the hearth and rolled up on all fours. She started toward me like a cat. "Suppose I want to seduce my Realtor and get royally fucked. I can just do it." Her face was inches from mine as she stopped in front of me.

"At what point does the Realtor get to say if he does or doesn't want to fuck you?" I asked.

"At any time before his cock is actually buried in one of my holes. From then on, it's too late. So, think about it quickly, because you don't have much time to decide." She closed the gap and pressed her mouth against mine. It wasn't just her lips. Her mouth opened, expecting nothing less from me. I opened my mouth in defense, hoping not to be devoured. There was nothing romantic about the kiss. It was a raw probing of each other with our tongues. I barely got my glass set down on the hearth before she had pushed me completely back, covering my body with hers.

"You had to know I wanted this when I invited you over to help christen my new house," she said.

"I suspected you might."

"And you showed up anyway."

"You are pretty tempting."

"Your silver-tongued negotiating got me a great deal on this place. Now I want you to put that tongue to work elsewhere." With that she stripped off her T-shirt and fell on top of me with her beautiful right breast pressed against my lips. It would have been ungentlemanly of me to refuse to pay attention to it. I raised my hand to cup her other magnificent tit and found her own hand already busy at the nipple, pinching and twisting. "Bite," she commanded. I nipped at the nipple in my mouth and was rewarded by her moan of pleasure. "Harder!"

I've always had an irrational fear that if I got carried away with a woman, I might bite her nipple off. Stupid, I know, but it is one of the things that makes me a gentle lover. I don't like to hurt people—or be hurt for that matter. But Allison had let go of her own tit, relinquishing it to my fingers and had slid both hands up under my polo shirt to begin tweaking my nipples. She wasn't being gentle and I had to assume she was giving what she wanted to get. I bit harder.

"Oh yes!" She twisted my right nipple hard and I bucked up against her as she ground her crotch against my cock. She dragged her right breast away from my mouth and shoved her left tit in. "Again!" I swear that when I bit down this time, her body went rigid in climax. She rolled off me and I raised myself up on my elbow facing her as she caught her breath. I scanned down her body, feasting my eyes on her perfect breasts. The nipples looked raw and red from my biting. The breasts didn't flatten out when she was on her back, which told me they'd been enhanced. I had a feeling as I looked closely at her, she'd had several bits helped out over the years—her perfectly straight nose, shining teeth, even her piercing dark eyes. She'd invested heavily in her body.

As I looked down toward her waist, narrow against the flare of her hips, I could see the crotch of her sweats darkened with moisture. I felt her pulling at my shirt and looked back into her eyes.

"Lose it," she ordered. By the time I'd pulled the shirt over my head, she had shed her sweats in one quick move and lay there completely naked. Her hands deftly unbuckled my belt and lowered my zipper as I stroked down her body and dipped a finger into the wet cleft of her pussy. It was impossibly smooth. The dark brown hair of her landing strip was neatly trimmed, not so short as to be prickly, but the rest of her delta was smooth. This was no shaving job. My cock throbbed as I imagined the beautician who had stared at this slit as she (or he) stripped the wax off. I realized my cock was throbbing in her mouth as she continued to push my jeans down my legs.

I rolled to my back so I could lift my legs and finish stripping off my jeans, briefs and socks at once. Allison rolled with me, never letting my cock out of her mouth. Taking the dominant position again, she drove my cock into the back of her throat and swallowed repeatedly, working her throat muscles around the head. She needed no instruction in the art of blowjobs. Firehoses be damned. This girl could suck the chrome off a '57 Cadillac. I was rising fast—much more quickly than I normally do. She lifted up and planted her smooth pussy over my mouth in a 69.

"Just bite on my clit when you come," she said. "I want your spunk shot directly into my stomach. Don't hold back. I want you to be able to last for the second round."

I couldn't answer because my face was buried between her legs and my cock was once again down her throat. I kept telling myself I wasn't into rough sex, but her dominance overwhelmed my resistance. She didn't need to wait long before I was spewing my load deep in her throat. I bit her clit just as I erupted. In fact, I bit it hard. Her legs shot out straight and her body went rigid, collapsing all her weight on my face and chest and driving my cock even deeper into her throat.

I gasped for breath, barely able to get my nose far enough out of her pussy to get air. She wasn't moving. As my cock began to soften, I felt no lingering action in her mouth. I rolled her off me quickly and as she hit the floor, the air exploded out of her lungs and she began coughing, flecks of semen spitting out of her mouth as she regained consciousness. My heart was thudding in my chest as I realized she'd suffocated herself on my cock when we came. Her eyes fluttered open and tears streaked down her cheeks as she continued to cough. I poured a little champagne into her glass and held it to her lips. She swallowed it, coughed again, and looked at me with a shit-eating grin.

"Oh god! That was good!" She hauled my head down and drove her tongue into my mouth, mingling her fluids in my mouth with those of mine that remained in hers. Her hand was back on my cock and, to my surprise, I found I was regaining my rigidity. It usually takes me a while to recover, but her hand was very persuasive. It left my cock for a moment and I broke the kiss to look down. She was collecting her own pussy lubricant all over the palm of her hand and when she returned to my cock, she smeared the slippery surface and stroked some more. She pressed her mouth to my left nipple and bit it. I screeched and pulled back, popping loose from the suction of her lips. My cock was rigid and I was just a little angry. I really don't like being hurt during sex. But my cock didn't seem to know the difference.

"Time for the main event," she said, rolling over onto all fours. "Shove that cock into my pussy and make sure it's good and slippery." I knelt behind her. God, what an ass! Her narrow waist flared out around the curve of her hips and tapered into thighs toned by God knows how many hours in the gym. Her butt was soft and full enough to belie the firmness of her thighs that were so tight they didn't come close to each other beneath her pussy. Her cleft and her rosebud were on clear display from this view. I was captivated by the vision in front of me. "I didn't ask you to paint it," she said impatiently. "Fuck it!"

I leaned forward and drove my rigid pole into her waiting and willing snatch. It was good that I'd just come so hard or I would have spewed out as soon as her pussy muscles gripped me inside. I began pumping in and out, reaching my right hand around her waist to play with her clit and my left hand forward to capture a breast. At least by now, I understood she liked it rough. I pinched the nipple hard between my fingers and was rewarded by her howl of pleasure and her butt slamming into my stomach. A fresh load of juices drenched my cock and the hand on her clit as she spasmed around my prick.

While she was still shaking from the orgasm, she turned her head back toward me and hissed, "Now. Shove it up my ass."

I pulled my cock reluctantly out of her pussy and placed the head against her very wet rosebud. Our earlier couplings had provided ample lubricant and I dragged my hand up through her pussy once more to smear her ass. I pushed gently against her back door, trying not to rush the experience. I knew from past lovers that ass-fucking is something that is done to please the man and most women don't get that big a charge out of it. It was a gift Allison was giving me.

I was wrong again. As soon as I'd begun to penetrate, she shoved back against me hard, taking the head and a couple inches of my cock inside in one move. At the same time, she yelled out in pain. I started to pull back, but she followed me with her ass, not letting me withdraw. "In! Push it in! All the way!" That's truly unusual. Even women who enjoy anal sex typically only want enough stimulation at the sphincter to get off. Having had my annual physical and getting probed with the Sigmoid device told me there were places up there that hurt when they were pushed. But Allison was relentlessly pushing back against me. She caught me slightly off balance and I rocked back on my heels. She used that as an opportunity to rise up on her knees and simply sit down fully on my cock.

"Ah! Ah! AH!" she screeched. She turned her head over her shoulder searching again for my mouth. As I kissed her, I tasted the salt of her tears streaming down her face. She was panting for air and as the kiss broke, she returned to her hands and knees and whimpered, "Now fuck it. Hard!"

Hard she wanted it. She was driving me crazy. How can I do something that would intentionally hurt her? But the more she pounded back into me, the more I lost track of who was in control.

If I backed off, she slammed back against me with another screech. I hunched forward, wrapping my arms around her waist and began hammering at her ass. She was incredibly tight and I was feeling some of the pain of dragging my cock in and out of her rectum. At the peak of every stroke, I could feel my glans hit the bend at the top of her rectum and she screamed in pain each time. The same bouncing pressure at the end of my stroke was progressively driving me closer and closer to coming. It drove my head further away from reason. I no longer cared if I was hurting her. I no longer cared if she had an orgasm. I was simply going to dump my load in her ass. My hips, with a mind of their own, drove harder and harder against her butt, burying my full length in her.

I reached forward with both hands to find her perfect breasts, drove my cock deep one last time, and pinched her nipples as hard as I could, twisting them left and right as my cock unloaded. The scream that tore out of her throat was almost drowned out by the bellow from my own. They echoed through the empty house.

That instant froze time. I was petrified in position with my cock buried to the balls, the scream from each of us seemingly endless. Spasms wracked both of our bodies. My cock drained the life out of me. We collapsed forward onto the rug, the action seeming to take forever before I came down solidly on her back. She lurched with her left elbow, driving it into my side so I would roll off. My cock dragged painfully out of her ass. She curled into a fetal position and cried.

I was devastated. I'd never hurt a woman. I stroked her shoulder. I leaned forward and whispered, "I'm sorry. I'm so sorry." In all my life, I'd tried never to say those words to a woman. Her shoulders shook and I thought she was sobbing more. As she rolled toward me at last, I could see that despite her tears, she was laughing.

"You would be. You're sorry you gave me what I wanted? Do you think you broke me or something? Do you want your come back? Well, help yourself. There it is, dripping onto the rug. You idiot."

"But I lost control. I didn't mean to hurt you."

"You like to be in control, don't you? A man like you never voluntarily gives up control. I had to make you lose it."

"But hurting you…"

"Don't you get it? Pain is just another kind of pleasure. You're such a fucking romantic. You wanted to make love. I don't need love. I don't want love. Don't be sorry for me. I felt something so intense it doesn't have a word to describe it."

"I'm not used to this kind of love."

"It wasn't love! And don't get used to it. I know you're an artist, Doc. I've seen your work." That surprised me. I couldn't imagine where she'd seen my work… unless she was friends with one of my clients. That would explain a lot. "Maybe someday, after I get furniture and have finished christening my house, I'll invite you over and you can show me what making love is like." She stood and I could see a big puddle of my come staining the new rug. I stood to get a paper towel from the kitchen to clean it up.

"Leave it," she said. "That's what I bought it for. I'm going to christen every room in this house with a different man or woman on that rug. Yours is just the first paint on my canvas."

I guess not all art is pretty.

7

# Pain is Pleasure

MY EXPERIENCE WITH Allison and the knowledge that my interlude with the lovely Rita was likely at an end left me depressed and angry. I'd been goaded into breaking all restraint and hurting a woman for pleasure. I didn't care about her pleasure in this instance. I'd hurt her for my pleasure. I couldn't face myself in a mirror when I got home.

I spent the rest of Thursday night and all day Friday in my studio. I usually have a lot of work to do on Fridays, preparing for the weekend open houses and placing ads. I took a break just long enough Friday morning to call Morgan in the office and tell her I wasn't well. I asked her to place ads for my two opens this weekend and told her I'd come in on Tuesday unless I'd landed a client. Then I silenced all my phones and went back to the studio.

I spent time with a sketch pad, first sketching out Allison's face. As I filled page after page of sketches, her face became more and more distorted in that excruciating combination of pain and pleasure she espoused. I sketched other parts of her body as I remembered them, sometimes adding piercings or tattoos to the drawing. I moved to a four-by-three-foot canvas and started sketching in the base for a portrait. I let the fireplace flames rage in the background as though they were a scene from hell. She said she wasn't asking me to paint her, but painting her was the only way I could express myself.

Against the flames, I began laying in the figure of Allison. I'd sated my desire to see her face, so the far right of the canvas barely captured her shoulder and breast, hanging below her. The arch of her back rounded into an impossible ass with her right leg disappearing off the bottom of the canvas so her gaping pussy could be clearly seen. On the left side of the canvas, next to her ass, an erect penis emerged from the flames pointed at her pussy, dripping fire from the tip.

Pain and pleasure. Pleasure and pain. I mixed paint and began to work, letting go of my normal control and adding flaming colors where I least expected. Damn if the reflected light on her breast should have come from the opposite side. I knew for a fact her nipples provided their own fire. As much as I'd lost control the night before, I lost it again in the color as I let pain and anger join lust and ecstasy on the canvas.

※

It's been a long time since I became so completely absorbed in my work that I lost track of time. I had to admit my painting lately had become mechanical, even commercial. I did portraits for hire. I painted models in classical scenes to be sold in galleries of decorating arts. I'd become stale. Now I was releasing something more from my brushes than my carefully schooled art.

The doorbell had rung half a dozen times before it finally soaked in to my consciousness. I left the studio to open the front door. I was shocked to find it was dark outside. Rita stood at the door.

"Rita! Come in! I didn't expect you tonight—not that it matters. You know you are always welcome."

"Thanks, Doc. You're covered with paint," she said, reaching up to kiss me.

"I was in the studio. I should clean up. I'll be right out and you can tell me all about your big date."

"Yeah. That's what I wanted to talk about." I didn't realize she was following me into the studio until I heard her gasp. I turned and saw she was standing in front of my nearly finished painting while I was at the sink ready to clean my brushes. She'd been in the studio before, but she'd never seen anything like this.

"I, uh… was just doing some painting," I explained. "It's almost finished."

"Oh my God! You got laid." There was no pact of exclusivity between Rita and me. In fact, she was supposed to be out seducing her former fiancé tonight. She didn't sound upset, so I wasn't concerned about sleeping with—fucking—Allison. I was surprised Rita seemed to jump to that conclusion so fast. Still, there is always a twinge when one woman realizes you are sleeping with another. I just wasn't expecting Rita's next words. "Finish it. I'll wait."

I couldn't deny I wasn't ready to quit painting. I'd been in the studio how long? I looked at the clock I keep for timing model sessions. It was ten-thirty. I'd come into the studio at nine last night after Allison had dismissed me. Dismissed. She had shoved my clothes into my hands and said, "Goodnight." I grabbed the brushes and palette and returned to the canvas, stepping in front of Rita. I fell back into my painting trance, renewed anger absorbing me into my subject. I didn't know if Rita was still in the room or had left.

Two hours later, I stepped back from the easel and returned the brushes to the mineral spirits for cleaning. I was exhausted. And hungry. It had been forty-one hours since I got up and I'd been sketching and painting with no more than a bathroom break for twenty-seven. Gradually the aroma of frying bacon and eggs reached my nose. I went to the kitchen to find Rita cooking.

"Sit down. You must be starving."

In the little time we'd been intimate—just over two months now—how could she know me so well? I collapsed at the breakfast bar and she shoved the food in front of me with a glass of juice. The bacon and eggs were cooked perfectly. I was shaking so hard, though, I could barely get the fork to my mouth. Rita moved beside me and gently held my hand steady as I fed myself. She didn't try to feed me or take control. She just supported my hand. By the time I'd finished enough food to stabilize my blood sugar, I was crying. My catharsis had finally come.

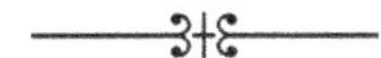

IN THE SHOWER, Rita cleaned the paint from my face and hands, shampooed my hair, and bathed my genitals—all while I clung to her and stroked her soft skin with my hands. Even with her gentle and sensual ministrations, I was too tired to become aroused.

We toweled off and she led me to bed, getting me settled before turning out the light and snuggling in next to me. She held me against her naked breast all night as I alternately slept and wept. I woke briefly the next morning to hear Rita on the phone. "He's not well enough to make his open houses today," she said. "Is there someone else who can cover? Thanks. I'll let him know. 'Bye." I didn't bother to protest. I fell back asleep.

THE NEXT TIME I woke up, I could smell coffee and that got me stirring. I used the toilet and washed my hands. I splashed water on my face, feeling an emotional hangover. When I stepped back into the bedroom, Rita was sitting up in bed holding a tray with two steaming cups of coffee. She was still naked, as I was, so I slipped back into the bed beside her and gratefully accepted the offered cup.

"Are you ready to talk about it?" she asked. I shook my head. "Then why don't I tell you about my seduction of Alex?"

I grinned at her. "That should be interesting. Not that I'm complaining, but why are you here?"

"Ah. That's part of the story. Everything went perfectly. The girls managed to ferret out the information about what bar he and his buddies were going to last night. So, we walked in about an hour after they got there. And did we look hot! I don't suppose you even noticed last night, did you?"

"Oh. I'm sorry. I was so dazed…"

"I could tell. I'm really looking forward to your story when you're collected enough to tell it. So anyway, what group of guys doesn't automatically turn to survey six gorgeous girls dressed to fuck? That mini I was wearing last night barely covered my ass. The rest of the girls were every bit as sexy. We were a perfectly matched set. Six girls, six guys, and Alex right in the middle of it. It took about two minutes for the guys to migrate to our table and buy our drinks for us. We made room at the table and even though Alex made a point of talking to Beth, he sat between her and me. I was pointedly ignoring him, but when Beth turned away to start flirting with his buddy, he didn't have much choice but to turn to me. It was that or get up and move," Rita laughed. "No choice."

"'So, how you been,' he asked. 'Fine.' I finished my spritzer and he called the waitress over to order a refill. 'Look, I didn't mean to hurt you…' I cut him off before he could go any further. I just reached over and put a finger against his lips like this."

Rita placed her finger against my lips to demonstrate what she'd done, looking deeply into my eyes.

"'Don't talk about what's past,' I said. But I didn't take my finger away from his lips right away. I just caressed them lightly. You know, men are such babies! He just opened his lips a little like he would suck on my finger. Then I pulled it away." She snatched her finger away from my lips and I realized that I, too, had been ready to suck it like a baby. She giggled. "Archetypes," she snickered.

"What then?" I asked, laughing at myself as much as at Alex.

"I ignored him. He had to make the next move, so he pushed back his chair and tugged at my arm to get me to follow him to the dance floor. He wasn't very subtle. It was a slow number and he pulled me against him. I let him polish his belt-buckle for a while as I felt his cock filling his jeans. When the number ended, I don't think he knew what to do. The next song was faster and Alex really hates to dance. I turned away from him and backed into him like it was an accident. I could feel his cock straining to get between my cheeks. I leaned back against him and whispered in his ear, 'You know why blue jeans are like a cheap hotel?' That took him by surprise and he just shook his head. 'Because there's no ballroom,' I answered. I reached back and stroked his cock. 'There's room in your car, though.' It took him about two seconds to get my drift and he wrapped an arm around me and practically dragged me toward the parking lot."

"Sounds like everything went perfectly," I said. I'd begun to get stiff just listening to her tell the story. I wasn't sure I wanted to hear about what happened in the car, but Rita had set her cup aside and was now turned toward me so her breasts just hugged my left arm. I could feel her hand floating on my chest and gradually drifting lower as she continued.

"Oh, he was hot and heavy right from the start. He was mauling my tits and trying to get his tongue down my throat. It wasn't seductive or gentle, so I had to take control. I pushed his shoulders back against the seat and ran my hands down to his belt. 'I've got something for you,' I said as I unfastened his pants and freed his cock."

By this time, Rita had shifted around to face me and was sliding down my body while caressing my cock. Her move was snakelike and mesmerizing. I felt the valley between her boobs envelop my meat as she slid farther down the bed, never taking her eyes from mine. Then she lowered her head and licked from the back of my balls to the tip of my prick in one long wet slide. I could see a huge drop of pre-come gathering at the tip.

"That's when it all began to fall apart," she said. She licked the pre-come from my cock and swirled her tongue around the head as she enveloped the glans in her lips. Then she gradually pulled back until just the tip of my cock was still between her lips. She gave it one more swipe with her tongue and lifted up to continue her story while she gently stroked me. "His pre was bitter. I don't mean a little on the bitter side. I mean so bitter it left the back of my mouth dry. Then I noticed his whole crotch smelled like shit. I glanced down and there was a brown skid mark down the middle of his white briefs. And his cock has this little bump on the side. I remembered that rubbing against the inside of my pussy and it was like a tickler put on sideways. It would scrape along the inside of my pussy walls, never quite in the right place to be a turn-on. It was gross to look at and I couldn't imagine putting it in my mouth. I kept stroking him as I looked up at his face and, for the life of me, I couldn't think why I thought he was so handsome. If anything, his face looked like a mannequin. You could have planted it on any plastic body and it would all be the same. I pulled back away from him and he reached to pull my head back down. 'Don't stop now, babe,' he said. I think he said 'babe' because he couldn't remember my name. I pushed more firmly away from him. I dipped a hand down into my panties and he said, 'Oh yeah, baby. Play with yourself." But I was just checking. I was dry as a bone. I looked at my fingers and then pushed farther away from him. 'You know what, Alex? You just don't do it for me anymore.' I flipped the latch on the door and left him there."

With that, Rita dropped my dick and turned away. All this time, she'd been stroking and demonstrating on me, and I was fully erect and waving in the air.

"You left him? Like this?" Rita turned back, pulled the sheet off me, and looked at my pole standing tall and proud.

"Mmm… Yep. Just like that. I ran to my car, jumped in and drove out of the parking lot. I didn't even bother to button up my blouse until I got here. The last time I saw him, he was getting out of his car with his dick sticking out of his pants, trying to chase me down."

"Why did you leave?" She turned back to me and gently began stroking my cock again as she planted a series of little kisses up and down my neck and shoulder.

"You told me once that I could turn on any man I wanted. But I realized I no longer wanted him." She slid back down my chest and stomach until she was once again stroking my erection between her luscious breasts. "I don't know how much longer I can keep coming here pretending I just want you to teach me things when what I really want is you," she said. She dipped her head, allowing her lips to engulf my cock as it emerged from between her breasts. "I want to explore and experiment," she continued, looking back up into my eyes. "But now, more than when I said it the first time, I want to learn how to turn you on."

I don't know if it was her open declaration, my recent experience with Allison, or a combination of both. I let my control slip away again. As she continued to slide her breasts cupped around my cock and look into my eyes with undisguised desire, I suddenly erupted, spattering both of us with come. A few spurts she caught in her mouth; some dripped from her chin and cheek and onto her breasts. As my climax settled, Rita glided back up my body and attached her lips to mine. I could taste my own rather bland spend on her lips and tongue. As she pulled back, I darted out my tongue and licked the come from her cheek, then shared it back in our next kiss.

"You know," she said. "I don't think Alex has ever tasted his own come. He wouldn't be so anxious to put it in someone else's mouth."

With that, she slid up just far enough that my still-hard cock could dip between her nether lips and into her very wet recesses. We made love for the rest of the day.

⸺ ❈ ⸺

DURING THE COURSE of the day and into the night, the story of my time with Allison came out a bit at a time. When I make love to a woman, I don't like to talk about other women, but Rita kept coaxing me to tell her what had upset me. Her eyes got big as I told her about the roughness. She was completely glazed over when I told her about the anal fuck.

We sat in the middle of the bed facing each other with our legs intertwined as I finished the story, telling her about Allison's equation of pain and pleasure and her determination to 'christen' every room in her house with a different man or woman. We had a bowl of grapes and berries next to us and fed each other. We kept stroking each other as well—my arm, her cheek as I fed her a berry, and yes, an occasional stroke along our genitals to make sure I stayed hard and she stayed wet. It was a beautiful view from my perspective as I could see her eyes, her lips, her breasts, and her pussy—all open and on display for me. She seemed fascinated with tracing the big vein that circles the side of my cock and crosses the tender underside. Her pussy lips had more wet highlights than would be believed on canvas. I was looking forward to our next round.

"Teach me," she said softly as she looked into my eyes. I shivered. I couldn't.

"I can't teach you about rough sex," I said. "It just isn't me."

"No." She glanced down and looked up at me under heavy eyelids. "Teach me anal. Your way. Soft and gentle. Not hurting me. Can you do that?" I smiled at her and nodded. "Do I need to get on my hands and knees?"

"No," I answered. "Stay right where you are. I want to be able to see your face and hear your voice. I want to know what I'm doing is what you want and that I'm not hurting you. We can do it face-to-face, like making love any other time. We just need some lubricant." She giggled.

"Do you mean what's been running down my crack for the past half-hour? There's already a puddle on the sheets." I slid my hand under her ass and slipped my finger up through her crack and into her bunghole. She gasped. She was right. Her rosebud was already slippery.

"Perhaps if I moisten my cock, it will be enough, but not to go in deep. The real pleasure for a woman is in the first inch or two, not the last six."

She leaned back and pulled my cock toward her pussy. "Here. Get good and slippery in here and then see what happens." I moved forward and my cock slipped easily between her folds, well-lubricated with both her juices and my own. We kissed. We made love, forgetting about the purpose of the session. I couldn't think of any sensation I would prefer over sliding in and out of Rita's pussy. Eventually, I pulled out and leaned forward to kiss her again.

"You guide it, Rita. Put the head where you want me to push. Slide it around and make sure everything is as lubricated as you can make it." She took hold of my cock with both hands and ran it through her slit repeatedly, making sure to spend time with my glans rubbing her clit. Her breath was coming in short gasps as she positioned my cock against her puckered asshole and began pulling me forward. "Take a deep breath," I instructed. She complied and held it. "Now exhale and let all the tension leave your body, including your butt." As she relaxed, I increased the pressure and just the head of my cock passed through her opening.

Rita's eyes popped open and I held still. "Oh!" I could feel her pulsing around my cock as her grip clamped down and she grimaced. I sucked on her left nipple—the one I knew to be most sensitive. When she gasped with the sensation, her sphincter relaxed and I slid in just far enough that I could make fucking motions an inch in and out of her ass. Rita emitted a long, low growl that sent shudders through both our bodies. She held her hand against my abdomen to stop any movement, unable to speak through her gasping breath. We stayed motionless like that for an eternity. I saw her eyes get big. She drew in a huge breath and then screeched out an orgasm without ever moving. The sheer force of her voice and fluttering of her muscles as she came sent me over the edge as well. The feeling of my cock shooting in her rectum set off another intense howl as both our bodies shook in climax.

I started to pull out, but she grabbed my cock and held it in place as her asshole squeezed and released repeatedly. At last, my softening dick was expelled from her rectum with one last squeeze.

Her eyes had never left mine, even in the intensity of our orgasms. Continuing to look at each other, our lips met and we fell together on the mattress.

# 8
# Sensory Deprivation

REAL ESTATE OPEN houses have two purposes. The first is to convince the sellers that the agent is doing something to market their house. The second is to get leads and new clients who are usually sold other houses. Only rarely—less than one percent of the time—does an open house result in the sale of the property being shown.

So, it was logical that on the one weekend I was too self-absorbed to sit at my own opens, a rookie agent with no listings of her own would clinch a deal for the house I listed.

That's not such a bad thing. It cuts my commission in half, but that's the half a listing agent normally expects to give to the selling agent. A seven percent commission is split between the selling agent and the buying agent. Of course, that half is split with the broker who holds the agent's license. Still, one-point-seven-five percent of $750,000 is over $13,000. Not bad. Especially since it was my second closing in 30 days. I would be banking most of it, just so I'd have something over the off-season in the winter. The chance of making a sale between November 1 and March 1 was less than half of the rest of the year. I knew agents who had separate businesses in Arizona and closed up shop in the North to spend the winter there.

On the other hand, my prospects for winter were looking up. After our soul-baring weekend, Rita had continued to come to me for instruction in the art of love, but as often as not, we simply met as lovers. We had made a deeper emotional connection. We hadn't had the talk yet—the one about the future and commitment. I'd been shy about committing to any woman since my college freshman girlfriend—who I thought I'd be with forever—left me. Oh, she didn't leave me during our freshman year. She left me the summer after graduation, exactly two months after our first wedding anniversary. I was shell-shocked at the time and almost missed my first week of graduate school because I hadn't emerged from my funk. The reason she was leaving me, she said, was that multiple orgasms on demand simply wasn't enough for her. Apparently, I got an 'A' in sex and flunked marriage. For the first time since then, I was allowing myself to become attached; it was a frightening though rather pleasant thought.

And so it was that we found ourselves in the studio one Saturday afternoon with Rita posing as my model.

The pose featured her as a woman clinging to her lover who was turning away. In order to get the setting right, I'd positioned a male mannequin facing three-quarters away from my chaise. I had Rita lie on her back and then twist her upper body to fling her arms around the mannequin. It was a delicious and erotic image when I just stood there to look at it. It didn't hurt that I'd positioned her with my hands, paying special attention to the exact position of her breasts and pussy. All the time, I'd given her strict instructions to stay perfectly still as I caressed her, just as her mannequin boyfriend did. I'd left her moist and panting as I went to my easel and began laying in the detail work on canvas.

"This would be a lot more fun if Studly here was better equipped," Rita said as she stroked her left hand up and down the mannequin's featureless crotch.

"Well, perhaps we can find a substitute for Studly when the posing is over," I said. This was our fourth sitting for this painting and I was about finished. "That's enough for today. I think we're pretty much done with this."

"Can I see it now?" she asked as she stood up and stretched. I clicked a mental photograph of that position. Her hands were stretched above her head as she went up on tiptoe and arched her body back and forth. I could almost see the scene in front of me.

"Yes, I suppose so." I hadn't let her see the development of the piece and wasn't all that sure I wanted her to see it now. I'd never felt uncomfortable showing my work to a model before. She padded over to me in her bare feet (and bare everything else) and looked at the canvas. I stood aside. Her brow creased. She tilted her head to one side in a reflection of the position she had held over the course of two weekends and four sittings. The expression on her face was not one of rapture.

"Uh… Doc… I know I'm not an art critic, but…"

"…but you know what you like," I said finishing the cliché that I'd heard repeatedly over the twenty years of my career.

"No. I know when something really sucks. This is terrible." The passion of her comment shocked me. After painting the canvas of Allison, I'd decided to do a series I'd mentally captioned Burning Love. I'd laid in a flaming background, repeating the themes from the earlier work with flame dripping from the cock. But Rita was not through with her scathing criticism yet. "Is that how you see me? With your artist's eye am I truly such a bitch? It's not just that it doesn't look like me, it's that it makes me look so awful! I don't ever want to sit for you again!"

"Rita. It's not a portrait of you. It's a portrait of something in my head. The model is just a reference point. I wanted to make a series out of the canvas I did of Allison. I don't think of you personally that way. Lots of artists use the same model for all kinds of works. Just think of Picasso. His mistress was his model but no one would suggest that his paintings 'looked' like her."

"You've told me about Picasso," Rita said. She was pulling her clothes on angrily—not just the robe she usually slipped into, but dressing to leave. "Where's that book?" I assumed she meant my book of Picasso. I retrieved it and she dragged me over to sit and look at the book. My style was nothing like Picasso, but I'd always admired his work. She began turning pages, focusing on the paintings of his famous model, Marie-Thérèse Walter, the mother of one of his children. "Look at these," Rita said. "They don't look like her but they look…" Her voice dropped to a whisper. "They look like he loved her." She looked over at my painting. "Not like that! You showed more love in your painting of Allison."

She left the book in my lap and stormed out of the house.

———⊰†⊱———

I OPENED MY eyes. I'd collapsed in bed after Rita left and just thought about what I'd painted until I was so exhausted from my own confusion, I fell asleep. I could see it. I knew what I'd done. I'd used Rita as a placeholder as I attempted to paint Allison again. And I hadn't done a particularly good job of it. My original painting had been free and uninhibited. This one was deliberate and controlled—exactly the opposite of what I felt when I painted Allison. It was an inappropriate theme superimposed on an incompatible subject. None of what I'd captured in the first painting was present in the second. Technique overrode passion. It was mechanical. There were flames but the painting was cold. That fleeting grasp of a breakthrough in my art now looked like an unhappy accident I'd never reach again. I would go back to the studio and scrape the paint off the canvas and prep it for another painting.

It was late but I still thought I'd go back to the studio. The room was dark. But something had awakened me from the dream of destroying my latest canvas. At first, I thought it was just an aftershock of Rita's tearful departure, but something else was nagging at me.

I heard a rustle in the room and reached to turn on my bedside lamp, but my hand was arrested by a soft but firm grasp on my wrist.

"Rita?"

"Shh. Trust me." It was whispered but I was sure it was Rita. She had a key to my house and often came in at unexpected times. I lay still, only moving slightly to help her remove my clothes. The one time I reached for her soft skin, she firmly returned my hand to my side. I couldn't figure out what she was up to.

She pushed me over onto my stomach and arranged my arms straight down at my sides and my legs straight out with my feet together. I must have rolled onto a fresh sheet as she tugged a folded edge out from under me and pulled the opposite edge over my back and tucked it in at my side. She rolled me onto my back again. I was effectively strapped in. I started breathing a little rapidly. I was sure I could get out as long as she didn't tie anything around me. But I didn't know what she planned. She'd been angry when she left. Was she about to take revenge on me? That simply didn't fit with her character. I was sure she had a purpose, but I couldn't still my racing heart. I relaxed slightly as she positioned a comfortable pillow beneath my head in exactly the way I like it when I sleep.

She next placed a sleeping mask over my eyes. It was heavy. A bag filled with some small grain like rice, slightly warm and not uncomfortable but sealing my eyes closed with no chance of a stray flicker of light impinging on my sight. I could see the color bursts behind my eyelids that always accompany pressure on the eyes—mostly reds and oranges with tinges of blue fading into the black at the edges. Gradually, the color subsided and there was no signal sent to my optic nerve at all.

Again, I felt her breath on my face as she leaned near my ear. I could feel the goosebumps rising on my flesh as the gentle breath blew across my neck.

"Trust me?" came the whispered voice in my ear again. This time it was more of a question than a command. A request for confirmation— for permission. I didn't say anything. I couldn't trust my voice to make the right sounds with my heart beating so rapidly. I merely nodded slightly. "Then relax," she whispered.

I felt a pair of earphones being placed over my ears. I moved slightly to get them comfortable, expecting to hear pleasant music or maybe a gentle voice through the headset lulling me to sleep. Instead, everything went silent. There was a very slight white noise stimulating my eardrum, but like the colors behind my eyes, I wasn't sure if it was from an external source or if it was simply my nerves filling in blanks that I normally wasn't aware of.

If you plug your ears with your fingers, you might effectively block out most of the ambient sound that surrounds us all the time. Sounds of the house, the furnace, the refrigerator, water in the pipes, outside traffic. You find these sounds replaced gradually by an awareness of your own internal sounds. Your breathing, the rustle of fabric against your hair, your own heartbeat. But the silence descending on me was complete. I couldn't hear my own body. I could hear nothing outside it.

And time was suspended.

I am an artist and, while that is not synonymous with 'drug addict,' I have had my occasional brush with mind alteration. There comes a point when smoking a little weed that time slows down. Or per-haps one's awareness of time is suspended. Everything moves in slow motion and until you emerge from your stupor, you have no concept of time's passage. You might be surprised when you look at a clock to find that hours have passed or that only a few minutes have crawled by.

As I lay in my bed with no more movement possible than a twitch of my fingers or toes, no sight or sound perceived, the same feeling of time suspension descended upon me. I had no idea how long I lay there. My heart rate and breathing slowed. I could no longer feel the thudding in my chest but assumed I was still alive. After I stilled my racing thoughts and relaxed enough to stop being curious about what she was doing, I discovered I was really quite comfortable. In fact, I drifted back into sleep.

———❧———

I awoke to featherlike touches on my crotch. I started, suddenly not sure if I was awake or simply lost in a dream of deafness and darkness. My heart started to race again when I realized I couldn't move. Just before panic set in, I remembered Rita's whispered words to trust her. I was in sensory deprivation.

I've dreamt before of losing my sight and remembered being in a huge cave once when the guide turned out the lights to give everyone an idea of what it was like to be in complete silence and darkness underground. The silence was short-lived as people began to shuffle and titter almost at once. But the darkness was complete and awesome. For a few moments, one's eyes played tricks and there was the impression of seeing lights, realizing it was nothing more than the retina being repaired and the optic nerve sending signals that originated before the lights went out. But those afterimages fade. The result, surprisingly, is not blackness. The rods and cones in the retinal layer continue to fire somewhat randomly, even in darkness. The result is what I can only describe as texture. I've tried repeatedly to capture that randomness on canvas, but something about the canvas itself and the reflectivity of the paint overwhelms the texture of the dark.

As I attempted to open my eyes beneath the mask on my face, I felt the lids scrape against the fabric. It was uncomfortable and resulted in no more light information than when they were closed. Rita was clever to use the rice or sand bag as a sleep mask. Its satin cover was gentle but unyielding when my eyelids fluttered and the compression of the grains molded the mask tightly to my upper face. There was no chance for light to leak in.

Even more startling, however, was the silence. When Rita initially placed what I assumed were noise-cancelling earphones on my ears I was intensely aware of the white noise that played through them. Waking up with them in place, however, I no longer had a ready point of reference for judging what I heard. I can only describe it the same way I describe the darkness behind my eyes. It was a textured silence. I sometimes have a bit of ringing in my ears—a mild form of tinnitus. In severe cases, people hear all kinds of random ringing, music, and even voices when fluids in the ear build up and apply pressure to the delicate hearing organs. I could hear nothing. As the old adage says, "I couldn't hear myself think."

My careful assessment of my vision and hearing had calmed my heart rate and I became increasingly aware of the feathery touches in my groin. At first, I thought I was imagining things and my fantasies were all that stimulated me. I applied the same focused examination of touch, however, as I had of sight and sound. Skin is the largest single organ of the body. In most places, it is about seven layers thick. The bottom layer—the dermis—contains the complex network of nerves that give us the sensory perception we call touch. The penis, however, has only three layers of skin, exposing the nerve endings to more direct and intense stimuli. Only the female clitoris and the human lips have more nerve endings than those in the penis.

Why does an artist know all this? We have to study human anatomy.

But it was all head-knowledge—and I mean the type where the brain is. With the blocking of my ears and eyes and the binding of all my body, it seemed the only sensations coming to my brain were coming from my cock. I was gradually gaining an erection.

Perhaps not so gradually, now that I was aware of it.

There seemed to be an opening in the sheet that bound the rest of my body because there was no restriction to my rising penis. It found warm air. I could define temperature, wind direction, and moisture from the sensations assaulting my cock. It was a regular weather vane. As it rose, I felt light soft touches, felt breath circling me, felt a gradual moistening of the glans. Amazing. Unless I'd used my hand (or someone else's), I'd never actually felt the pre-come seeping out of my cock. Now I could tell it was there by the temperature change when she breathed on me.

When her hand gently grasped me, I was aware of the exact position of every finger. My mind immediately jumped to the assessment that it was her right hand. It was dry but soft, gliding in a circular motion around my cock with the thumb starting next to my abdomen and twisting to the underside as her fingers glided around. Then her left hand joined in. First, it was just the flat of her palm pressed softly against the opening where my pre leaked in a steady flow. Rather than stroking up and down, her hands kept up the twisting motion left and right—fingers and thumb at the base and flat of the palm at the top.

I'd always known stimulation of my nipples could be felt in my cock. It is one of the most pleasant sensations a lover can provide. I can only assume the same response in a woman since licking a nipple often leads to moistening of the pussy. What I'd never felt before, though, was the tingling in my nipples resulting from the stimulation of my cock. I could feel my nipples harden beneath the sheet as my prick distended to an impossible size. Of course, I had no actual reference to compare its size with my normal erection, but it felt like it was filling the universe. I lost myself to the sensation and didn't attempt to restrain myself when my orgasm shook my entire body with such intensity that I couldn't breathe for several seconds.

Another new sensation wrapped me up. This time a warm moist cloth gently bathed me and I felt the coarse fabric in opposition to the unbelievable softness of her hand. When the cloth was taken away, my penis cooled rapidly in the air as the water evaporated until I felt her breath closing in on me and the tip of my penis being sucked tentatively between her lips.

She went at it slowly. Since our night of instruction, Rita had progressed into a fantastic fellatrix. Someday, I thought, I'd have to write a thank you note to her former fiancé. I saw a flash of color behind my eyes as I thought of her and felt her warm lips caressing my erection.

⸺ ȝ⊹ɛ ⸺

I HAD NO idea how long this blowjob had been going on. Her rhythms were irregular. She would suck a while, bob her head a few times, and pull back to stroke again. I never really softened after the first hand job, much to my amazement. She was doing an incredible job of keeping me on edge without letting me come again. There was nothing I could do but lie there and take it. Bound in the sheet as I was, I couldn't really even thrust. I occasionally tightened my pelvic muscles a little and was rewarded by feeling the head of my cock expand in her mouth, but she often pulled back when she felt this. I calmed myself and let her do the driving. I had so much come built up, though, my eyes were leaking behind the sleep mask.

Then her mouth seemed to harden. Her tongue was tighter against my cock and she slid farther down on it with little bounces that kept jostling her head and mouth down on my cock. She was coming! I'd had my cock in her mouth when she came on occasion but I guess I was so caught up in my own satisfaction that I'd never noticed how her mouth and tongue felt when she came. One hand gripped me more tightly as her mouth continued to throb around my cock. With the sudden intensity of feeling her orgasm, my cock exploded into her throat.

I don't know whether she swallowed, held it in her mouth and spit it out, or just let it run out of her mouth as I came. It made no difference at all. My release was so sudden and hard that I blacked out for a moment. I don't know how long I was out. I awoke to the sensation of having my cock bathed with the warm wet cloth again. I was still hard (again?) and the soft washing was followed by yet another tongue bath. Another flash of color behind my eyes and in the back of my mind an image began to take shape. I lost it immediately when she straddled me.

I could tell by the pressure against my arms her feet were toward my head, which meant she was in a reverse cowgirl position. Her hands continued to stroke me, making certain I was hard. She stroked the head of my cock through her slit and ran it around her clit. It was a delicious sensation, but I realized I was being given a lesson as well. She was showing exactly how she wanted my cock to stroke her, how long she wanted me to wait before plunging in. A wonderful reversal in the student/teacher roles. Without saying a word, I was learning more about how to pleasure Rita.

She brought my cock to her opening three times before she began to slide down on me. She couldn't have had more than a couple of inches in her when she stopped. Her hand still gripped my cock outside her pussy and I thought for a moment she was pulling off me as I felt her rise until only the head was still in her. Then her hand released me and she suddenly plunged down on my cock all the way. I jerked my upper body forward, bending at the waist, nearly dislodging my blindfold.

This wasn't Rita.

I'm not a connoisseur of pussies, meaning if you lined up all the lovers I've had in my life and I inserted my cock into each one, I would be unable to tell which pussy belonged to which lover. But I would be able to tell differences between them—differences in depth, tightness, texture, and occasionally, an oddity. This pussy had an anomaly I'd never felt when fucking Rita.

Well up inside her vagina, there was a bend or fold such that when I was fully seated in her, I could feel the ridge pushing against the left side of my cock. I froze in position and forced myself to lie back and return to my sensory deprived state. Who was this? I couldn't think of a lover I'd had who felt like this and was at a loss to think what friend Rita might have brought to share me. She'd asked me to trust her. There wasn't much else I could do. I wasn't going to shout out that I didn't want a strange pussy lodged on my cock, though my racing heart was telling me to panic.

I was bound, deprived of sight and sound, titillated under false assumptions, and fucked. In other words, had I not acquiesced to trusting Rita, I could claim to have been raped. A war raged in my head over whether to be offended by Rita's betrayal of trust, or to be thankful to her for introducing another—and now that I considered it, quite delightful—experience for us to share. All through this inner battle, the lover hadn't moved. She simply sat on my pole with her butt firmly against my abdomen.

I've seen men's cocks that when aroused point out at a ninety-degree angle from their bodies. I point up and to the left. The skin on the top of my penis is simply much tighter than that below and it pulls me upright, so fully erect, there is only an inch or two between my penis and my stomach when I'm standing. As a result, the reverse cowgirl position pulls me forward and down. When at last she rose and plunged onto me again, she pulled me even farther forward and

I scraped along the inside of her channel almost painfully. It seemed she was working her clit up and down along my shaft as she began to rise and fall, slowly at first and then more and more quickly. The mild pain due to the distension of my cock kept me from approaching an orgasm myself, even through her first and second climaxes shuddering around me. I could feel her hand reach down to cup my balls and then stroke up along my shaft until she reached her clit, where I could feel the vibration as she rubbed quickly.

I disconnected my higher thought processes—what were left of them—and decided to simply enjoy the ride. I started to bend my knees so I could thrust up against her, but they were firmly pushed back down to the bed. I was supposed to be a passive recipient of this sexual experience, not a participant. When I'd relaxed my legs back down flat, my partner seemed to relax as well. She leaned back with her hands behind her and began sliding more vigorously up and down. This released some of the downward pressure against me and I quickly began to mount toward my own climax.

It was then I received the next confirmation that this was a two-person act. I knew her hands were both beside me from the pressure against the bed and my arms, but another hand began caressing my nuts and playing with our joining. I was trembling from the nearness of my climax. Finally, I felt a tongue at our joining and it vibrated as it flicked against my partner's clit and back against my cock. After only a few of these flicks, my lover began to convulse in orgasm again, tripping me over the edge as well. Even after two climaxes previously during this encounter, I was still pumping enough fluid out my penis to dehydrate me. She seemed in no hurry to disconnect and leave, holding me inside until my spent tool finally softened and slid out of her of its own accord.

I was bathed again, my cock kissed repeatedly—in fact, so often I began to wonder if it was only two women or if Rita had invited her entire whine and dine group. But my cock was no longer rising, even with the thought of six women worshipping it. At last, there was a single pair of lips that slipped over the glans, gave it a soft suck, and let it pop out of their grasp.

Then there was nothing.

———— 3†8 ————

I LAY THERE waiting. I may have drifted a bit as I tried to understand the images playing behind my eyes and the sounds I thought I should be hearing. I thought about rolling over and releasing myself but couldn't work up the energy to do it.

Finally, I felt hands move back to my crotch, but instead of grasping me, they tugged the sheet wrapped around me. It tore from little head to big head, suddenly relaxing the pressures against my arms. The headset canisters were removed and I heard the softest of whispers against my ear as the flood of house noises came rushing in on me.

"Now, go paint," she said. Then I was alone.

# 9
# Out of Body

I WAS AWAKE, RESTED, showered, shaved, and fed. It was a considerable advance from the last time I'd had such an emotionally draining studio session. And I was happy.

I'd pulled myself out of my cocoon after Rita left and headed for the bathroom. When I opened the door, I smelled freshly brewed coffee. There was, however, no sign of Rita or my mystery date. I poured a cup of coffee and headed directly to my studio. I didn't bother to dress. I have several workspaces in the studio, set up to let me work on different kinds of paintings and sketches. I sat in a comfortable chair, set the coffee on a table, and pulled a small sketchbook and soft pencil out.

I started small, trying to capture the essence of what I'd felt in the night. Sensory deprived in all but my cock. I had no control over the use of it. Even my one attempt to thrust had been rebuffed. And behind my blindfold, my eyes painted explosions of color into the darkness. In two hours, I'd moved to a larger sketchpad and the remaining half cup of coffee was cold.

I set up my easel with large sheets of rough paper and experimented with charcoal as I drew sweeping curves. The figure leaned back toward the left of the paper, just her chin showing below the upper left corner of the sheet. Her throat extended as her head was thrown back, arching into the line of her breasts. It narrowly missed the feeling I wanted. As I looked at it, I saw the problem. I'd drawn shadows against a white background. I needed to draw light. The sudden burst of imagery I saw behind my eyes as we exploded together.

On a large sheet of Bristol, I laid in a full-page background with the flat of a 4B soft graphite block until the entire page was covered. Then I pulled out an Art Gum eraser and a tortillon and began erasing the parts where highlights would burst out of the shadow. As I saw the shape emerge from the shadows, my heart began to race and adrenalin pumped into my veins.

I prepared a canvas, changing from my initial concept of a horizontal image to a square image. As I worked, I absently chewed on a sandwich and drank coffee without bothering to wonder how they had materialized in my studio. My mind was filled with the image and I could do nothing but focus on my painting. The rough sketch flowed onto the canvas and before I had even finished it, I began laying in the background. The figure would bisect the canvas diagonally. The man below her would be a faint suggestion of a dream-lover, penetrating her depths. There was just enough detail to suggest the act without being explicit. The torso twisted to her right, facing the artist slightly. Her right hand extended down to grasp at the darkness with her fingertips as the left arm was flung across her breasts, raking passion out of her ribs.

But most of all, there was the palpable texture of the darkness surrounding the figure. Each color I worked into the highlights was muted into near transparency against the pebbled Payne's grey background. I painted that texture as if my eyes were closed and I could sense the pinpoint of each rod and cone firing to create light and color on my retina. Paint flew across the canvas and much of the area that surrounded me as I let go of the fine control of figure drawing and let the light be born from the darkness.

That was the theme. That was what I truly captured. Light borne of darkness. It was as different from the painting of Allison as it was from any of my other work, yet it was a complement as well. In one painting, flames of passion threatened to consume the figure and all it touched. In the other, passion seemed to arise from the ashes, coalescing them into lover.

I took a deep breath and awareness gradually dawned on me that I was still naked, having come directly from my bed some twenty-eight hours ago. I was spattered with paint, and I sported a rigid hard-on as I looked at my painting.

———⊰⊱———

I SPENT MONDAY cleaning my house, changing the linens on my bed, and eating. Periodically through the day, I found myself giggling uncontrollably. As pained as I'd been when drawing and painting the canvas of Allison, this canvas had left me high as a kite. Around noon, I sent a text message to Rita that said simply, "It is finished." Even that made me giggle as I noted the religious connotation. Half an hour later, I received a response: "We'll be there at six to see. Let's have Chinese."

That was all it took. First, "we" were coming to see the painting. Rita was bringing my model—secret lover—with her. I would see her with my eyes for the first time. And we would have dinner. At five-thirty, I ordered from a local restaurant and went to pick it up. I arrived home just minutes before Rita pulled into her drive, followed closely by a late-model mid-class import. A conservative car, I noted as I set the table and dished steaming rice, soup, chicken, and vegetables into serving dishes. I watched from my vantage point inside to see who would step out of the vehicle.

Rita went to the door of the car and opened it, carrying on an animated discussion with whoever was in the car. The occupant seemed reluctant to come out. I debated whether or not to intervene by opening the front door, but this was Rita's show and I was determined to let her control the way it played out.

Finally, the figure emerged from her vehicle. She was professionally dressed in a dark suit with short-cropped dark brown hair. She stood a good two inches taller than Rita and, though she was fully dressed in a shape-concealing business suit, I was certain I could have recognized her even if I'd merely glanced at her on a street corner. My eye superimposed the curves and the elongation of the torso from my painting over the figure of the woman who now approached my door.

"Doc, I'D LIKE you to meet Dr. Kelly Thompson. She's my…"

"Colleague," Kelly broke in. Rita beamed. I was pretty sure Rita was about to say 'boss.' I instantly respected Kelly for her separation of work hierarchies from her afterhours relationship. She immediately held out her hand and I took her firm grip in mine. I nearly giggled again.

"Dr. Kelly, I'm Dmitri Peters," I said.

"Doc," Rita broke in.

"I'm not a real doctor," I said. "I have an MFA in art. I can't be Doc in the presence of someone with a degree."

Kelly laughed. "Over the past few months, I've heard Rita talk constantly about 'Doc.' If you don't mind, I'd be happy to just be Kelly and let you be the doctor. I can't quite think of you as Dimitri." Kelly's laughter was infectious. I was already thanking Rita in my head for bringing this woman into our lives. I ushered the women to the table and we began eating, carrying on the normal chit-chat of new acquaintances.

I learned Kelly was the lead researcher on a project at Rita's company and, while they had become good friends, they seldom worked directly together. Rita was the research assistant on a parallel project and they often found themselves in adjoining labs at odd hours. None of us mentioned the events of the weekend or the artwork waiting in my studio. Nonetheless, I was fully convinced Kelly had been the model, the secret lover, and the inspiration for the work. I was a bit nervous to find out her reaction.

I served coffee and the three of us moved to the living room. I sat in an armchair and noticed Rita and Kelly sit next to each other on the sofa. It's a large sofa—Rita and I first made love on it just a few months ago—but the two sat closer together than was strictly necessary. Nor was it an aggressive act. Neither sat at the end with the other encroaching on her space. They sat as a couple in the middle. I thought I detected more than a friendship between the two.

"I've a confession," Kelly said.

"It was my fault," Rita broke in.

"We have a confession then," Kelly corrected.

"I ran an experiment on you without your permission," Rita jumped in.

"Rita explained to me what she had in mind and I jumped at the chance to help her," Kelly added. "But I have to say I was selfishly motivated. If you are upset, please direct it at me rather than at Rita. As the senior researcher, I didn't exactly follow protocol. I used you."

"Please," I said. "Let's not level any blame until you've seen the results. I'm not particularly upset. Although the circumstances were, shall we say, unusual, I did give Rita my assent and trust. I was surprised but not displeased."

"It was all about creating a safe way for you to be out of control," Rita said. "It didn't go quite the way I'd expected. I kind of lost control myself."

"Well, as far as control goes, I'd say we all suffered a degree of loss," Kelly said. "But Rita, dear, I need to put things into perspective for Doc. After all, I…" She hesitated and I moved to ease the way for her.

"You became my lover and inspiration," I concluded. She grimaced at the words and I wondered what was up.

"Not exactly," Kelly said. "That's what I need to clear up. I am not your lover, nor are you mine. You see, I'm not exactly turned on by men." Now that was a surprise. The raw passion I felt sometime in the middle of Saturday night was certainly not that of a lesbian as far as I could tell. Kelly reached over and grasped Rita's hand, scrunching her eyes closed before continuing. "I joined Rita Saturday night as a scientist. Although her experimentation base was questionable, she'd described her intent to me in such a way that I agreed—no, I volunteered—to come and record the experiment." She must have seen my eyes pop open at that because she hurried on. "Not on tape. Oh God! That would have been unconscionable. I was just taking notes. It gave me a sensation of voyeurism that was unbelievable."

"What moved you from being an observer to becoming a participant?" I asked. "I have to say, none of the sensations I felt that night led me to believe you weren't fully enjoying the experience."

"Oh, yes. I was. But what moved me, as you say, was Rita. I've been attracted to Rita for some time, but I knew she was truly heterosexual. Even though she described various experiments she'd done with you, it was obvious she was not trying to entice me. Until this weekend, our relationship has been strictly professional at work and strictly as friends outside. But as I watched her… In your room… And she undressed… I was distracted. I just wanted to touch her."

"God, did she ever!" Rita exclaimed. "You have always told me about how all your senses work together. You want to see me, hear my voice, touch me, taste me, and even smell me when we are making love. You want to be connected in every way you can. So, I set up the experiment to see if I could get you to respond, even when all your senses were isolated. I focused exclusively on the bundle of nerves between your legs. My intent was to get you turned on without letting you see or hear anything—without letting you respond with any part of your body except your cock. I'd stay away from your mouth because I know kissing is one of your biggest turn-ons. For our purposes, I couldn't do much about your sense of smell without introducing some other scent. So, I just had to go with that as an ancillary factor. If I was doing my thesis on this, I'd have to set the whole thing up in a lab, but I wanted you to be completely unable to control the experience and thought it would be better to surprise you with it than set it all up with you in advance."

"I trusted you," I said simply. "That is what you asked. And it proved the right decision."

"I was watching and, for a while, I thought you weren't actually going to respond," Kelly said. "I thought that was amazing because

I'd always assumed men had a basic disconnect between their brains and their penises. But what was really getting to me was watching Rita. She was worshipping you. She was so beautiful and so sensual and so arousing that I couldn't help myself. While she was still lightly stroking you and attempting to arouse you, I stepped up behind her and began… touching her." Kelly's voice broke a bit on that last word. "Before I knew it, I was just as naked as she was and I was worshipping her body as much as she was engaged with yours."

I wasn't sure what to do with the information I was receiving. I wondered if somehow during the night, Rita and Kelly had become lovers and I was now out of the picture, so to speak. But Kelly wasn't finished.

"She guided my hand the first time I touched you. We were kissing the first time you came. My other hand was stroking her beautiful breast. I was so surprised when I felt your sperm spattering against my hand that I almost bolted from the room, but Rita… While she continued to stroke you without pause, she raised my come-covered palm to her lips and licked it clean. She was so thorough, so caring, so loving as she licked my fingers, sucking each one into her mouth that I came. Hard. I thought for a minute I'd ruined her experiment and you would know I was there but the ear and eye blocks she put on you seemed to be holding. I thought perhaps you had passed out. Regardless, from that point on, I was actively involved in the experiment instead of recording notes."

"It was quite an experience," I said. "I didn't realize there was more than one person until you mounted me."

"When you started to sit up and brought your knees up, I knew you were aware. I was afraid you would call it off. If you'd said something besides 'Oh!' we would have stopped," Rita said. "But since you didn't, I decided to make it obvious and join in. I had originally intended it to be me on you."

"What made you decide to do something like that, Kelly? You said men didn't do it for you." Kelly hadn't let go of Rita's hand, although I was beginning to sense a little discomfort on Rita's part. I wasn't sure yet what was going on between them.

"I prefer women. Exclusively. But when women get together it is not unusual to use toys for pleasuring each other. With you wrapped up like you were, I could ignore the fact you were a man and treat your cock as if it were a dildo and Rita was my lover. When she added her tongue to the equation, I lost all sense of having a living man inside me until I felt you pulsing in me. That was better than any dildo I've ever tried."

"I think I understand," I said.

"You do?" Rita asked.

"Sure. Men do absolutely nothing for me, either." Both women laughed and some of the tension went out of the air. "Really. There is nothing about a man that turns me on. I'm not repulsed by them but I don't find myself checking them out in the gym showers or looking forward to a guy taking off his shirt in a movie."

"That makes sense," Kelly said. "You are just a normal heterosexual man, right?"

"Yes, except I wouldn't hesitate to cross swords with a guy who was trying to get into the same sheath," I responded. "I might even help a guy out to get him up and into the woman we were making love to. I'm not squeamish about semen or afraid of cocks. They don't turn me on, but if I were in the same position with you that we were in the other night and it was a guy who was licking my balls and your clit instead of Rita, I'd still come just as hard. The thing is, it's the girl we are both focused on that makes it a turn-on. The guy just happens to be part of the package."

"Or has the package," Rita giggled. "I think I understand, too. Kelly, I really like you and I've known for a long time you find me attractive. I guess I wouldn't have asked for your help if I didn't have some desire to show off for you. But I'm not gay and I don't think I'm even bi. The casual girlfriend hugs and occasionally holding hands for security…" she held up their joined hands, "…is fine. But women just don't turn me on. It was the two of us working on Doc that tripped me over the edge. Seeing, up close, Doc's cock in your pussy was what brought my tongue into play. I can't imagine I'd do that if it was just the two of us, any more than I think you'd suddenly want to make love just to Doc."

Kelly looked down at their clasped hands and seemed to be a bit embarrassed. She loosened her grip and started to pull away. I decided it was time to move things along a little before this precious opportunity was lost. I left my chair and scooted in on the sofa next to Rita. I laid my hand on top of Kelly's before she could fully pull it away.

"Did you know about my lessons in the art of love with Rita?" I asked. Kelly nodded her head. "And are you still wanting to run experiments on me, Rita?" Rita nodded. "Well, Kelly, it seems we have a great deal in common. We are both turned on by our lovely assistant Rita. It seems we should be able to cooperate in her seduction, don't you think?"

"You'd still want me with you, even though…?"

"I don't make a practice of trying to seduce lesbians," I said. "I understand as much as is possible for me that it is part of your being and not a choice. I wouldn't try to convert you. But your sexual orientation doesn't prevent me from being turned on by you, just as Rita's heterosexual preference doesn't stop you from being attracted to her. We could do some serious tag-teaming with this young woman and, if during the course of action, you decide to use my 'dildo' as well, you can simply think of it as an appliance in Rita's arsenal." The said Rita was wiggling between us as we both leaned in toward her. Her eyes were glimmering as she glanced between Kelly and me.

"I'm pickle in the middle!" she exclaimed. Kelly and I laughed with her and each planted a kiss on her cheek.

"I have to say, I wouldn't mind another ride on the only cock that's ever been in my pussy," Kelly said, blushing.

"What?" Rita and I both exclaimed at once, turning to stare at the rosy face of the research scientist.

"I've always been a lesbian," Kelly said. "Until that impulsive moment Saturday night when I impaled myself on Rita's dildo—I mean your cock—I'd never had a man inside me. I just kept thinking, 'Oh Rita! I love your girl-cock.' And now, I kind of wish she'd push it into me again."

# 10
# Girl-Cock

W E'D ALL HAD a little chuckle over Kelly's statement but in the wake of it, everyone got shy. Kelly let go of Rita's hand. I stood up and went for a fresh bottle of wine. Once everyone's glass was filled again, we sat staring at each other.

"Well, shall we go look at the result of the experiment and judge whether it was an artistic success as well as a social success?" I asked. "I admit, after my last failed attempt, I'm anxious to have your opinion of this one."

"I'm sorry I was so huffy about the other one," Rita said. "It was so hard to look at that painting and think you saw me like that."

"It was an artistic failure as well as a personal one," I said. "The whole piece looked like I was copying someone else. It was mechanical and had no depth of feeling. I should have known better, but was too buoyed up by my success with the first painting."

We headed into the studio where I directed them first to the painting of Allison. I'd decided to call it *Pain is Pleasure*. Kelly hadn't seen it yet, so I wanted to prepare her for the kind of painting I was doing now. I was not yet sure what I'd call the painting of Kelly.

"That is hot!" she said. "I mean, not only the flaming hell that surrounds her, but the passion she shows. She ignites the painting with the torment in her soul." I was impressed. I had no idea what Kelly's experience with art was, but that she went directly for the emotional impact rather than style or technique was definitely a point in her favor.

"The rawness of the emotion… The exposed nerve endings… That was what I was hoping our experiment would reveal," Rita said. "There's also a sense of loss of control. Doc can paint a technically perfect portrait, but you can see the control in every brushstroke. You know, even when you were 'teaching' me how to be seductive, it was you who seduced me. You controlled the entire scenario."

"I'm sorry about that," I said. "I guess I did get a little carried away."

"Don't be sorry! It was a wonderful introduction to the art of love. I haven't regretted a moment of it since that night."

"Ah. But we're scientists," Kelly said. "We want to see the results of our experiment." I moved them over to where they could see the fresh easel and pulled the cover off the painting. "It's me! I'm beautiful!"

A quick shift of position had Kelly sandwiched between Rita and me as we hugged her. She was transfixed, just staring at the picture.

"I love the way the light and color just emerge from the darkness," Rita said. "You couldn't see any of that but still it came out in your painting."

"And the figures… I mean you can tell they are having sex but you can't tell where one ends and the other begins. It's like one is rising from the other. Kind of an out of body experience," Kelly said. "In a way that's exactly what it felt like to me. I was having an out of body episode."

"Good title for it," I said.

The hug turned into a kiss as Rita leaned in toward me, I leaned into Kelly, and Kelly leaned into Rita. After a moment of sorting out our noses, our lips and tongues each found two others to join with. In a few minutes there was no doubt left as to where the evening was going. We adjourned from the studio and landed hard on my bed as every person's hands were full of another person's clothes, attempting to get them off so our skin could touch as we continued to tongue-wrestle among ourselves.

While a little shy at first, Kelly proved to be every bit the researcher that Rita was. She wanted to examine my anatomy and had to stifle an urge to get paper and pen to take notes. She asked what positions Rita and I had experimented with and gasped in horror when Rita told her about her experience with anal penetration. Then Kelly examined Rita and pressed a finger first against Rita's anus and then against her own to see if they were similar or if Rita was more accommodating of an insertion.

The women further subjected themselves to my examination as I talked through a comparison of each of their features. Kelly was a good two or three inches taller than Rita. Her dark brown hair was a subtle contrast to Rita's not quite blonde, light brown hair. Her figure was slight, a little thinner than Rita, though not unpleasantly so. There was no roundness to her belly as there was with Rita. And Kelly was shaved bare compared to Rita's neatly trimmed bush.

"I suppose you knew it was someone other than me when you didn't feel any hair," Rita said.

"Mmm. At the time I wasn't really thinking coherently enough to identify the difference between a bald pussy and a hairy one with only the head of my cock as input. I didn't actually realize it wasn't you until Kelly sat all the way down on it."

"I'd gone halfway," Kelly said as she reached out to tentatively stroke my shaft and then circled her fingers around it about three inches below the tip. "Rita was guiding it inside me and I almost panicked and started to pull back. Then she kissed me and I just slammed myself down. The feeling sent me over the edge for the second time that night. I had to just stay there in one position while Rita kept kissing and stroking my breasts." Her hand slid off my cock and she dreamily pulled Rita into a deep kiss, stroking our lovely assistant's breasts.

"That was when I knew it wasn't Rita," I said as I dipped my head between the two and licked the beautiful nipples pressed against each other. Rita's areolae were tiny and almost transparent against her milky white skin. Her nipples rose in a hard swell that was only a couple of shades darker. I thought that if it were not for the delicious mounds on which they were perched, her nipples would look almost like a boy's.

Kelly, on the other hand, had a darker complexion than Rita. Her larger areolae and prominent nipples dwarfed Rita's. But it was obvious that both women found the caresses of my tongue on their touching nipples to be very stimulating. "When I went all the way into you," I continued, "I felt the difference between your pussy and Rita's. You have a little fold in your vagina that I could feel against the side of my cock. It was very pleasant."

"You can actually tell the difference between pussies when you are in one?" Rita exclaimed. "Which did you like better?" That is a question one never wants to answer!

"Rita, darling, unless there is something drastically wrong with a pussy, there isn't a man alive who would compare it and say better or worse. Men just want different, not better."

"Well, Kelly had you last. It is definitely my turn." Rita lay back on the bed and Kelly followed her down. Rita spread her legs for me, but Kelly had her left leg draped over Rita's waist as she latched onto a little nipple to suckle. As I guided my cock into Rita, Kelly's opening drove back against my hip as well. I slipped my hand between us and began stroking the lesbian's very wet slit and love button. Her hand slid beneath her leg to tickle at Rita's clit and our joining.

We all tried to keep it slow, but the build-up and long period of kissing and petting we'd had was driving all three of us closer to release. I slid a finger up into Kelly and used my thumb to apply just a slight pressure to her anus. She skyrocketed. I could feel her fingers tighten on Rita's clit and suddenly Rita's muscles were clamping down on my cock and sucking the juices from my balls outward. All three of us screamed our release.

As we lay in our first panting heap of the night, Kelly asked, "Is it different when it is in you from the front instead of from the back?"

"Oh, yeah!" Rita exclaimed. "I understand why you wanted a rear entry, because you didn't want to engage with Doc. But when we cum face-to-face, with our eyes open and looking at each other, it is so intimate and so much better."

Kelly rolled over on her back and pulled Rita toward her.

"Give me your fresh-fucked pussy to suck on while you drill me with your girl-cock," she whispered. She was talking to Rita, but she glanced up at me and bit her lip shyly, looking questions at me. I nodded, more than willing to comply. For her part, Rita was willing enough to help me make love to Kelly. I waited until her pussy and ass completely blocked Kelly's view, then I dipped my head to take a long wet swipe along Kelly's slit. I heard Rita scream.

"Oh! Do that again!" Rita called out. I dipped my head and licked at Kelly once more and Rita squealed. "I can see you do it and I can feel it at the same time. Wow!" I got it. Whatever I was doing to Kelly, she was repeating on Rita. I thrust my tongue into Kelly's twat and Rita moaned. "Oh! So deep." I flicked Kelly's clit a few times with my tongue and inserted a finger in her pussy. Rita squealed and I could see past the mounds of Kelly's breasts that were grasped firmly in Rita's hands. Kelly had a hand wedged up beneath Rita and had three fingers buried in the girl.

I slid up Kelly's body and gave a gentle lick and suck to each of her nipples as Rita pinched them into points for my tongue's ministrations. I kept going, licking up Kelly's chin and toward her busy tongue. Rita got the point and leaned back, supporting her weight on her hands so she didn't completely suffocate Kelly. With my chin against Kelly's, our tongues met, caressing each other and rising to tease Rita's clit together. I continued the journey upward and when I started sucking on each of Rita's delicate nipples, my cock was aligned with Kelly's opening. I was thinking what a great thing this would be to have an endless chain that I could work my way up—pussy clit breast breast pussy clit breast breast—but as I thought this, my cock gave a twitch against Kelly's clit and her hips jumped forward to slide me in. I drew Rita's mouth to mine in a gentle kiss as I sank slowly into Kelly's depths. This time, I could hear the slightly muffled scream as Kelly clamped down on my cock and Rita's clit at the same time. Rita stiffened, moaning into my mouth.

Feeling both women cum was stimulating, but I wasn't ready to let loose yet. I figured Kelly wasn't going to have this experience often and I wanted to make it as special for her as I could. I began stroking in and out of her slowly and felt Rita stiffen in front of me again. She pushed away from my face far enough to moan out, "Oh. My. God. I have a tongue in my pussy and a tongue in my mouth at the same time. Ohh!" Rita suddenly wrenched herself away from me and off of Kelly in one motion. "Too much! Too much! I can't take any more!"

Her sudden movement sent me forward, burying my cock even further into Kelly. I could feel the little fold stimulating the side of my cock and it was driving me on. But when she felt my chest touch her nipples, Kelly's eyes flew open and she looked directly into mine. I could see a moment of panic and was ready to pull out and away, but Rita came to the rescue, diving between the two of us and planting a hot kiss on Kelly's lips. Kelly relaxed and began driving her hips up to meet my thrusts. Rita slid to the side a bit and whispered "It's okay, Baby. Just relax and enjoy my big old girl-cock. You can enjoy everything you want to and no one is going to think a single bad thing about you."

Kelly smiled and opened her eyes again. At first, she focused only on Rita, but her eyes slid to mine. I smiled at her and then felt her hand against the back of my head. She pulled me to her lips and we kissed, slowly at first, then deeply as our joined bodies moved more and more rapidly toward the precipice. Rita slid in closer to us and insinuated her tongue between our lips. My right hand caressed Rita's butt as my left held my weight and all three of us kissed together. The ripple that began deep in Kelly's cunt seemed to run up and down my cock in waves. She looked deeply into my eyes as she opened her mouth and silently screamed her orgasm.

That was all it took to send me over the edge as well and when my come began splashing against Kelly's cervix, the silent scream became vocal. I felt Rita's hand between us and knew that in addition to my cock's stimulation, she was manipulating Kelly's clit with her fingers as the three of us dove into another searing kiss. Then we began to come down. I didn't attempt to move or pull out until Kelly's grip on the back of my head relaxed and finally fell away.

At midnight, we were still cuddled together with Kelly on Rita's right and me on her left. We did no more than pull a sheet over ourselves and fall asleep.

# 11
# Adoration

REAL ESTATE IS a tricky business. The old joke is that an agent spends his commission three times—once when he gets a client, once when he makes the sale, and once when he gets the check. As a result, most are behind in the earnings game. I learned early on to live within my means. That was more of my father's teaching. He sat down in a very businesslike way and pointed out that as an agent, I had no monthly paycheck to depend on. Therefore, when I made my first sale, I needed to consider it my income for the year and budget accordingly.

Now, each January, I determine what my budget is for the rest of the year and put my commissions in the bank to cover the months when there are none. In spite of the recent real estate collapse, I'd done pretty well for the past fifteen years. That included making sure my accounts were all balanced for the year before taxes were due.

The inevitable fall slow-down had begun early. I had closings well into October, but by November 1, my inventory was low and the prospects for listing were decreasing. It was time to 'fill the pipeline,' in real estate parlance. That meant getting clients on board so as soon as the weather breaks in the late winter, we have houses going on the market. Occasionally we get a mid-winter bonus.

That's what happened when I listed the Morrison house. Ed Morrison had accepted a transfer with his company and was moving out East. He'd found housing there and the family planned to move after the winter holiday. Most folks don't like to move their kids in the middle of a school year, but the Morrisons were more concerned about keeping their family together than keeping it in one place. If Ed was going to be in Pennsylvania, then so were the rest of them.

It was a good house, too. I paid for the appraisal myself before setting the marketing plan. I'd negotiated with Ed regarding the initial asking price and we'd decided that going over a million would be a killer in this market, so we settled on $949,000. I already knew they would take as much as fifteen percent less than the ask but the trick would be moving the house during the holidays.

As it happened, the office got its normal fall class of freshman real estate agents, fresh out of the necessary classes and newly licensed. Dan, my broker, was holding the licenses and wondering how many of them would still be in the business by spring. I've known Dan since I entered the industry myself. He's a good guy, if a little crude at times. Seems he's always interested in figuring out who the cutest new agent is and then getting it on with her. It's always a little sad when we look at four new agents and know only one of them will still be with us at this time next year.

"How about we do something new for this class," I suggested. "You know I just landed the Morrison house with a full seven percent commission attached. You and I don't really need that commission as much as these newbies need a sale. Here's what I propose. Let's make the full commission a six-way split if the house sells inside the agency before the first of the year. That will put six of us on the line for marketing, getting prospects, and holding opens. If any of us can get it sold by Christmas, we'll each walk away with one percent and the lucky person who closes the deal will get two percent. Everybody wins."

"Except me," Dan groused. "You'll be within half a percent of what you would get as the listing agent anyway. I'm giving up two-and-a-half percent for the benefit of these kids."

"Mmm. Jackie is no kid, if you noticed. She's a good bit older than me. But think of what it would mean if they all got a payoff for working together. We could have more than one of them still with us by June."

"I'm not saying 'no.' I'm just making sure you know who is really paying for your noble idea. You get to set everything up. They are now officially your mentorees."

I wasn't sure that was a word. I'd had a really good year, not the least of which was helped along by my lovely assistant Rita and the new style of painting I was doing. Nothing to do with real estate but it made me feel good. I called our four new agents together and laid out the proposal to them. The first thing they wanted to know was what was wrong with the house that I was willing to give up part of my commission to get rid of it. I explained the situation as best I could without sounding too altruistic. The truth was I'd been contemplating getting my broker's license and setting up on my own. It was even on my goals sheet for this year. It would pay me personally if I knew there was some bright talent willing to go with me. I couldn't really say anything about that to either the agents or to Dan. Instead, I said there weren't many houses to practice on during the holiday season and I was on a personal project that would limit my time. I let them know I'd run dry on ideas to market the place during the holiday season and would like some fresh, untainted input.

Just putting out that much of a suggestion deflected the questions from my motives and people started tossing out ideas for marketing the house. I suggested a field trip and everyone packed up to go look at the house. I decided to let them brainstorm a little more and didn't go with them. Instead, I headed back home to my studio. There was something nagging at the back of my mind.

———ॐ———

My team of rookies came into the conference room looking extremely proud of themselves Friday. They'd spent the entire week researching and writing their marketing plan. Dan and I sat in the room and waited for them to get organized. Alan took the lead.

"We are launching in a single big event weekend," he started. "Our goal is one hundred visitors to a triple open house, Friday, Saturday, and Sunday of Thanksgiving weekend.”

I saw Dan drop his head and I shook mine vigorously. There was so much wrong with this idea.

“Oh no. It’s a holiday. We’re talking about Black Friday. Everyone is out shopping. Who’s going to come to an open house?”

“Exactly,” Alan said, as if I’d just figured out their strategy. He reminded me a lot of what I was like when I started in real estate. He was young—in his twenties—determined, and energetic without the manic tone that so many young real estate agents get. I’d once had a twenty-six-year-old agent come to me so hyper I thought he was on drugs. He spoke so fast and so excitedly that he sprayed my desk with saliva and I backed my chair as far away as possible. Alan, however, was intense but not out of control. Even as a new agent, he was also working on his MBA. I waited to hear him out.

“We want to hold the opens on Friday, Saturday, and Sunday evenings.”

“Evenings?” This was getting worse all the time.

“Yes. Here’s the plan. The Morrison House is in exclusive Holly Park, a gated community that makes holding open houses difficult because there is no drive-by traffic and people can’t get into the community.” I nodded. That was one of the major problems of market exclusive homes. Typically, one couldn’t use open houses.

“Except, on four weekends a year,” Jackie took over. “Holly Park is known for having the best holiday decorations and light display in our region. They open the gates and allow traffic through on Friday, Saturday, and Sunday evenings between Thanksgiving and Christmas. Hundreds of cars come through the community on carefully routed one-way streets. So, our proposal is to extend the opening weekend of the lighting displays into the inside of the Morrison house. If we can get ten percent of the visitors to stop and tour the house, we’ll have over 100 potential buying parties. That’s over ten times the number that come to a normal open house.”

"What about traffic considerations?" I asked. I was beginning to warm to the idea but could see a huge traffic backup if people were parking instead of driving by.

"I checked with the president of the neighborhood association and with the local police," Bob said. He was about 30 and had knocked about after high school, not having high enough grades to get a college acceptance that he could afford. After working in various warehouses and a season or two doing construction, he went back to get an AA degree at the local community college. He followed that with the training to get a real estate license. He was a big guy and built like a rock. He was a little intimidating for real estate sales, but once you got to know him, you saw he had a rather sweet personality. "The police send a contingent of volunteers out that keep things moving while the gates are open. All streets are one-way during the tour hours. You enter at one gate and leave at the other. The Morrisons have a big circular drive with enough width to park on one side and pass on the other. We're thinking we hire a couple of high school kids to direct traffic in the driveway and make sure no one drives in if there are no spaces available. That will help keep the inside traffic manageable as well. We realize not everyone will get to see the house, but even if they don't it might drive calls for appointments during the daytime."

"I see this bringing in a lot of looky-loos and not many qualified buyers. Any plan for that?"

"A leaflet campaign in other affluent neighborhoods, including other residents in Holly Park," Alan said. "We'll also promote the decoration tour at the Executive Club and to several corporate headquarters in the region with an exclusive invitation to tour the Morrison house. We've also decided to greet people at the door and do a quick qualification and collection of names and addresses before they are allowed to follow the plastic-lined path, which is also a one-way route. That way we can keep people moving and have people stationed every so often to keep an eye on things and make sure nothing disappears."

I looked at Dan and he had a kind of half-grin on his face. He just raised an eyebrow at me. It was my show.

"It sounds like you've thought this out well as a team. Ron, I haven't heard anything from you yet. What are the downsides?" Ron was a quiet guy and I figured it was possible everyone else might have just railroaded him with the idea. He always dressed in a conservative suit, white shirt, and tie that made him look older than he was. I guessed barely twenty-one or twenty-two tops.

"I can't work evenings on the weekend," he said softly. "It's family time. I went into real estate so I could set a reasonable schedule that would let me spend time with my wife and little girl. I think the ideas the group has put together are good, but I can't participate. I'm going to have to withdraw from the group and try to make it on my own."

"Hey, Ron," Jackie said. "We don't want to lose you on the team. Heck, half this idea was yours. Why didn't you tell us you couldn't do the evening things?"

"It all seems like such a good idea," Ron answered. "And after I brought up a suggestion, I couldn't very well shoot it down. I planned to do Saturday work, like I agreed with my wife, but I never thought about the evening thing."

"You are all going to be shot after spending so much time at the house in the evening. Consider putting Ron on phone duty in the afternoons to answer questions and set appointments for private tours. The best prospects want another showing," I said. "I don't see any reason an evening limitation should prevent full participation on the team."

"I agree," Bob said. Jackie and Alan nodded. From there on, the event had a life of its own. These guys had a heap of work to do before they could open the doors at the Morrisons', and they needed to recruit some other workers for the event.

———◈———

I WAS INVITED to spend Thanksgiving with Rita at her grandmother's house next door. Miriam, the grandmother, greeted me with a smile.

"There's really no sense in pretending you two are just next door neighbors," she said. "If you are going to act like family, I'm going to treat you like family. Now come in and open a bottle of wine." I gave her a quick hug and kiss on the cheek. When I entered the kitchen, I was greeted by Tina, Rita's younger sister. Not alike at all!

Tina's husband, Rick, was in the living room with the television on and the Macy's parade entertaining their six-month old baby. Tina had married her high school sweetheart, supported him through college and then settled down to raise a family. Rick had graduated with a degree in electrical engineering and went straight to work for a software development company. I'd sold them their first home. Tina was still carrying a bit of extra weight from the baby, but she'd never been thin. She was designed and built from the ground up to be a mother.

"Doc, it's great to see you again. We love our house!" Tina said. I think she'd said that every time I'd casually passed her when she visited her grandmother. "We redid the nursery just before Rachel arrived. She loves it. Especially the rocking chair. I spend hours in there reading to her."

"I'm glad the house is suiting your needs. I think you got a good buy on it."

"Yes. It will be fine to get us through number two, but we'll need to get a bigger house before we have more babies after that." I guess Rita was spot on when she suggested she'd leave the breeding to her sister. It sounded like Tina intended to have enough for both of them. I grabbed the corkscrew and opened one of the bottles of wine I'd brought. Tina set three glasses on the counter for me to pour and went back to tossing a Caesar salad.

"Um… Five adults, Tina? Who's not having wine?"

"Oh, Rick and I don't drink alcohol. Never have. I joined the Mormon church before we were married so we could marry in the temple. We prohibit alcohol and are discouraged from drinking coffee or tea. I still drink tea to be sociable," she said. "I don't mind, though. You all can have wine and coffee. It doesn't bother me."

That explained a lot. I knew the LDS church was reputed to be a great place to raise children and encouraged married couples to bear fruit. I'd look forward to getting Tina and Rick a new house as their family grew.

Rita looked into the kitchen. "There you are! Has my evil sister seduced you away from me?" she asked.

"Rita! What a terrible thing to say. I'm quite happy with what I have, thank you," Tina reprimanded her.

We clinked our glasses together and I said, "Here is to everyone being happy with what they have. Cheers!"

———3†8———

LATER IN THE day, I saw Tina, Rick, and little Rachel cuddled on the sofa as she fed the baby from a generous tit. I wished I had a sketchbook with me, but I snapped a mental photograph. It was a picture of pure love. The baby looked up into the eyes of her mother as she suckled, an expression of adoration on her face.

"Are you looking at my sister's tits?" Rita whispered. She nudged me with an elbow and I pulled her into my lap.

"No. The baby. The family. I need to sketch."

"Okay. I'll be by after a while." She stood up and pulled me up by the hand. "Doc has a huge event this weekend and needs to go prepare for it."

"Thank you for a lovely Thanksgiving together," I said. Miriam reached up to give me a hug.

"Any time, Doc. You are always welcome."

———3†8———

I SKETCHED.

By the time Rita stopped by, I had a canvas on the easel and was laying in the washes. She brought me a turkey sandwich and fixed a fresh pot of coffee for me. Then she disappeared.

It was a smaller canvas than some of my more recent paintings, just twenty by twenty inches. And it was a closer view that I'd carefully cropped in my mind. The focus was on the baby. And the breast. I

97

couldn't have one without the other. No other faces entered the picture. It was Tina's breast and Rick's hand touched the baby's head. Otherwise, it was a portrait of Rachel, the little girl who looked at her parents adoringly. Adoration. That was the title.

I worked all night. That was becoming a common theme when I entered this painting trance. Rita brought me breakfast and fresh coffee. She stared at the nearly completed painting. There were no fancy techniques or trance-induced flinging of paint in this portrait. I just tried to capture the moment of intense love. The baby concealed the nipple in her mouth and most of the areola. Her little hand patted the breast she suckled. I'd painted detail that I didn't remember seeing when I watched the scene. The freckles across the top of Tina's breast. The slightly crooked index finger of Rick's right hand. A curl of Rachel's nearly black hair, plastered against her ear. A spit-up cloth tossed over Tina's right shoulder. It was all in the painting, along with the intensity of the six-month-old little girl.

I lay my brushes aside and put an arm around Rita. She sniffled and I saw tears running down her cheek.

"My sister is so lucky," she whispered.

———3∤8———

I'D DISCUSSED THE plan with the Morrisons and they approved it whole-heartedly. So much so that they went all out to decorate, inside and outside the house. It was truly a showpiece. We carefully laid plastic runners along the path people were to follow when touring the home. Even as tired as I was after painting all night, I was there with the four rookie agents, preparing the house for showing all afternoon. Mrs. Morrison and her daughter were so enthused they baked cookies all afternoon. The aroma of the decorated cookies and a crock pot of hot spiced cider wafted from the kitchen where people could pause in their tour to talk to one of the agents. It was a festive atmosphere all around. The Morrisons left the house just before five so they didn't have to witness the crowds descend.

It was a bit slow for the first hour before it was fully dark. Every house in the exclusive neighborhood was lit up with holiday cheer. I guessed many of the displays had been purchased from and installed by professionals. As high as my opinion of the Morrisons was, I couldn't imagine that many people in their class would do so much work without hiring someone. Call me a cynic.

By six o'clock, there was a non-stop stream of people pulling into the driveway and touring the house. The numbers began to taper off by nine and at nine-thirty, we closed the drive and refused any more new guests admittance. At ten, the last guest left and the Morrisons returned to their home. We were all tired and I told the crew I'd see them the next day. When I got home, Rita was there to relax me and sleep cuddled next to me.

What a wonderful assistant!

—— ֍ ——

AFTER THREE DAYS, we'd hosted two hundred buying parties, maybe five hundred individuals. For our purposes, we were interested in the groups, not the individuals. If a family of five comes in, that's still just one buying party. We sorted leads, ranked by interest. Even after discarding those who just wanted to see inside one of 'those homes,' we still had twenty serious parties in the market for a new home. More than half of those weren't qualified for a property this upscale, but there was a good possibility we could match them with something else.

Two lucky agents roped contenders and by Wednesday, we had a bidding war. I had to stay out of the picture since I was clearly representing the seller. By the time the week was over, the winning bid was $1.15 million. Closing was set for December 30. Five happy people would get a check for $11,500. Bob would be starting the new year with a check for $23,000. We were definitely in a mood to celebrate.

Personally, I intended to take most of the remainder of the year off. The niggling idea I had when we got started on this project was still in the back of my head and I needed to be home to paint. I was also hoping Rita would be able to take some time off. Maybe we could go skiing. Regardless, I was taking a working vacation.

## 12
## Spin Class

SKETCHES WERE LAID out in front of me all over the studio. My laptop was playing a slide show of my paintings as I sat back and just looked at what I'd been producing. I hadn't realized what was happening to my work until the past few months when I'd done three paintings that stood out from the rest. My work, all technically good, had become… I couldn't think of any word but 'commercial' to describe what I was doing.

I'm not ashamed of that. Some of the great artists over the centuries had supplemented their work with portraiture, graphics, and even decorating. Hell, Thomas Kinkade had made a career of being the 'Painter of Light.' His company estimated that one in every twenty American homes had a Kinkade painting or art print. My work had evolved to a point where it wasn't really worth anything else. I painted nice, sexy portraits of nude women to give to their husbands or boyfriends. Or to hang in their apartments. I didn't paint museum pieces. But that wasn't how I wanted to see myself.

Not until I painted Allison.

It was a stark shift. The computer screen lit up with the portrait I'd done of Sheila. It was a technically perfect snapshot in oil of a beautiful rich lady. But that was as far as it went. If I donned the persona of an art critic, I'd have to say the artist was … bored. The next painting that came up on screen was the flaming hell portrait of Allison. I now called it *Pain is Pleasure*. It was as if two different artists had put the color on the canvas. I couldn't say it was an exact likeness of the woman. Even if it had been, it was unlikely that more than a couple of people could have recognized her from this angle. It was a portrait of anger and abuse and violence. For all that the flames leapt around her body, it was obvious the woman was not the victim. She was the source of the fire.

The screen changed again to my painting of Kelly, now titled Out of Body. Again, not a photographic portrait. Somehow, in fact, this image was less related to the woman herself and more to the dreamlike attachment to the male beneath her. In neither of the two portraits were the faces of the women visible. In fact, I'd never seen Kelly before I painted it, even though she claimed to recognize herself as soon as she saw it. But the portrait was about release and abandon. She seemed to rise out of the dreamer in an ecstatic wisp that took on a life of her own.

The screen changed again and I was so filled with tenderness that I nearly wept. I called the painting of little Rachel at her mother's breast, Adoration. The only thing that showed of Tina was her milk-filled boob. Only Rick's hand on the baby's head indicated his presence. But the look in that baby's eye was one of absolute worship for her mother.

I had to decide if I wanted to continue down this path and how to do it. My attempt to superimpose Rita's image in the theme of hell had backfired dramatically. It came up on screen and I shuddered, looking over at the blank canvas I'd scraped the paint off and repainted in a white base. I was still unwilling to make another attempt at painting Rita. I wondered, though, if I was going to need a spiritual experience with every model in order to paint her as freely and gain the emotional connection of these most recent three. I'd had two other clients in the same period and I did portraits they were proud of. Me, not so much. I'd had no connection with them.

That's why all the sketches were strewn about on the floor of my studio. I was looking for a subject I could connect with. There were a couple I kept coming back to. I remembered clearly the sitting with Sheila. Yes, we had been sexually intimate, though without the final consummation of intercourse. And then there was the money left behind the screen. A tip. I'd shoved the five $100 bills in the first Salvation Army pot I'd seen. That was a year ago. When I was licking her, I imagined she was a passionate lover with her husband, and perhaps her massage therapist, personal trainer, tennis coach, and others. But when she'd been satisfied, she simply turned over and offered to let me fuck any of her holes, but to hurry up with it. It became a cold transaction and I realized it was not the artist who was uninterested, but the model. The coldness. The ice. That was what I was seeing as I looked at the sketches.

I started sketching again.

She'd taken the last two sketches I'd done with her to 'give to her husband,' she'd said. Did he get off on her offering herself to other men? Those were the images seared into my memory. The proffered ass. The open pussy. The frigid coldness that radiated from her, freezing anything within range. It was early in the week. When Rita stopped on Friday night, she'd have a new painting to look at. I hoped.

When I began to prepare a canvas, I turned off my phones. I knew I wasn't going anywhere for a while.

❊

"It's… Wow! It's beautiful and horrible at the same time," Rita said when she got in after her usual girls' night out on Friday. She looked and I could see her absorbing the painting. "Who is it?"

"A client I did a portrait of about a year ago. Just about the time you and I were getting together."

"But you didn't fuck her. And this can't be like the portrait you painted then."

"How could I fuck her? Look at it."

"She was really that cold?"

We stood and looked at the painting together a few minutes longer. I'd discovered I didn't need to be out of control. I'd shown that first in Adoration. This confirmed it. I thought back to the day when Sheila had decided to unnecessarily pose as I painted her portrait. I'd enjoyed

102

her intentional seduction of the artist. And I'd enjoyed eating her. She was involved when I was giving her pleasure. But when I realized what she was doing—after I'd eaten her to orgasm—I declined the offer to fuck her. I don't just take an offered fuck to have a place to stick my dick.

The painting, on the same canvas I'd scraped of Rita's image and prepared fresh, was of a banquet table, spread with food and wine. It was almost reminiscent of a Renaissance still life. But in the midst of the table, I'd painted a woman on her knees, back arched and head thrown back. Her hair hung off her left shoulder. Her hands were raised and clenched in orgasm as she howled out to the skies. You could see right through her in places; the reflection from her glossy surface showed a blue candle flame.

The food at the outer edges of the painting looked real enough to eat. The food closer to her was covered with frost, ice crystals glinting on wine glasses, and silver flatware. The only clue that she was not simply a perfect pristine ice sculpture in the middle of the table was her left knee, resting on a plate, cracked down the middle.

"Like ice," I said.

Christmas was pleasant. I was once again invited to Miriam's house for a family dinner and exchange of presents. I watched, as I'd done every place I went since my last painting, but no new scenes presented themselves to my imagination. At Rita's suggestion, I decided not to show *Adoration* to her sister. We didn't think the painting would appeal to either her or her husband.

Then Rita and I took off for a ski vacation at a Colorado resort. I made a lot of sketches, but hadn't found an inspiration among the snow-clad peaks or bundled skiers at the resort. Which is not to say I wasn't inspired in the bedroom. I'd fallen well and truly in love with my lovely assistant Rita. When we returned, we'd discussed the very real possibility of her moving across the driveway from her grandmother's house to mine. I'd not lived with anyone since my ill-fated marriage back in college. Rita's most recent experience was the sour end of her engagement to Alex.

We decided to take it slow, though more and more of Rita's clothes were in my closet.

———⋇———

I HAD OTHER things to worry about, as well. I'd given my entire referral list for the Morrison house to my four rookies as I took most of December off. Their pipelines were filled with enough follow-up to keep them busy for the next three months. I had nothing in *my* pipeline.

I put off finding a new subject to paint and spent some long hours in the office making calls to former clients and asking for referrals. I was determined to show the newbies what it takes to really succeed in the business. I hit the pavement with New Year calendars. I knocked on doors in neighborhoods where I thought there were good potential listings to be had. If it was up to my effort, I'd turn the housing market around by myself. But, of course, the market wasn't as strong as my effort and all I could do was lay the groundwork to build my list for spring.

———⋇———

I HEARD THE doorbell sound its warning but before I could move from my comfortable chair where I was reading a risqué website I'd discovered, there was a knock and then the rattle of a key in the lock.

"Doc?" Rita called. "Doc? Are you here?"

"I'm right here," I said from the top of the stairs. I'd long since given Rita a key but she usually knocked or yelled out when she entered the house. I'm not sure if she felt she needed to warn me she was in the house so I could sneak someone else out, or if it was just her insecurity about being welcomed whenever she wanted.

She rushed up the stairs and into my arms. Her hair was straggly, as if she'd been sweating. Her normal business clothes were askew. She must have thrown them on quickly. It was unusual to see her on a Monday evening. We'd had a nice evening Sunday. It was even more unusual to see her after work in less than a professional demeanor. I wondered if she'd been in an accident or attacked.

"Are you all right? What happened?"

"Doc, how much hot water do you have?"

"It's an on-demand water heater. It doesn't run out," I answered. I'd had the house re-plumbed about five years before and an on-demand system was high on my priorities. I hated to run out of hot water when I was in the shower or to not have enough hot water if I was doing dishes, laundry and a shower at once.

"Shower. Now," she said as she dragged me by the hand to the master suite. I'd converted a five-bedroom three-bath house into a three-bedroom two-and-a-half-bath house over the years by extending the master suite into one of the bedrooms for a dressing room/closet. I'd changed the back-to-back full bathrooms into one huge en suite and one public three-quarter baths. The house was built before the age of bathrooms the size of Texas came into vogue and I'd indulged myself with a more luxurious bath than was required. The only thing my bedroom lacked was a fireplace.

Rita shed her clothes as we rushed to the bedroom. In the marble covered bathroom, she turned on the double-size shower with all hot water and then turned off the fan. She tugged my clothes off almost as fast as her own had been dropped. I caressed her bare skin and began thinking of things we could do in a hot shower. I was more than a little worried, though, about what had inspired this sudden need for a shower.

"Hot," she said. "We need lots of steam in the room." I adjusted the shower heads so the hot water wouldn't fall directly on us. It was much hotter than the usually-regulated 110 degrees normally recommended. She dragged me into the shower and we sat on the low marble bench that ran the full width of the shower. It had been one of my inspirations when talking to the contractor. He'd mentioned a client who wanted a shelf built into her shower so she would have a place to put her foot up while she shaved her legs. I thought that was a brilliant idea. Plus, I could imagine all the other things one might do in the shower if there was a full width bench in the shower. Unfortunately, there had been few opportunities to explore the possibilities since the remodel was complete. I hadn't imagined using it as a steam room.

Rita pushed me to one side of the bench, careful not to get under the direct spray of the hot water. She slid to the side opposite and leaned back against the wall to put her right foot up on the bench while her left trailed off the side. This position left her breasts and her pussy delightfully exposed to my eyes, though the steam in the room was getting thicker by the minute. I adopted the same pose opposite her.

"I have to tell you what happened," she said, just above the sound of the running water. Her voice had turned from urgent to husky. She was still breathing heavily.

"Mondays, after work, I go to a spinning class at the club. That's what keeps my butt in the nice shape you like so well," she giggled. "It's a class that has very uneven attendance. One week, every bike will have a rider and the next week, only two people show up. It's weird. The instructor doesn't even notice. She has her workout routine set and she follows it whether there are two or twenty. I'm not sure she even looks up to see how many people there are. She just shouts out instructions for changing gears and taking hills as she buckles into her own workout. You would think someone named Gabriella would be heavenly and ethereal or that she'd be a down-home gal you'd call Gabby. But she's neither."

I tried to imagine this Gabriella but I was so distracted by the visual image I saw through the steam, it was hard to concentrate. The shower—the whole bathroom—had filled with steam and Rita continued to sit opposite me with her right knee up, letting it sway back and forth a bit. This caused her pussy to gap open and closed as her knee moved. It was hypnotic.

"I went to class this evening after work. Got to the bike room and I was the only one there when Gabriella started barking out orders like the room was full. Somehow, I think she took some bizarre pleasure in making me work even harder because I was the only one there. I groaned when she announced 'we're going to do hills.' I put my head down pumping away and the terrain keeps changing. She was pushing her settings out to the bike I was on and I was supposed to keep up with her. The forty minutes were hell! I've never worked so hard in my life and I thought I was going to collapse by the time we went into cool-down for the last ten minutes. Then she just said, 'Good ride,' and left."

It didn't sound like a good time to me. Nor did it explain why she came here to get showered and cleaned up after her workout. Rita is not that interested in being seen in public if she is not perfectly put together. But she wasn't finished with her story. The steam in the room shifted with a bit of air current caused by the running water and I could see Rita's right hand creep across her belly. She lightly stroked the neatly trimmed hair of her pussy, her knee continuing to rock back and forth. I felt a stiffening in my member in spite of the heat.

"By the time I'd dragged myself into the locker room, it was seven o'clock. No one else was there. I suppose the rest of the after-work crowd had already done their workouts and left. I regretted having gone to spin class and decided I'd just relax for a while. After a quick rinse in the shower, I soaked in the spa and then decided I'd take a steam before I finished off the evening with another shower."

I understood the rush to get home after work. I'd been putting in a lot of hours at the office lately and usually came home too exhausted to do more than heat a dinner and veg out.

"It was in the steam room that things got interesting," Rita said. "I found a spot just to the right of the door in the corner. The benches surround the room on three sides with the steam jets on the door wall. I went to the upper level of benches because I could lean against a wall and not against the board of another bench. I was sitting there, just like I am now. It was dreamy. I got to thinking about some of the things we've done over the past few months and it was such a comfy steamy room, I just started stroking my pussy a little bit. I remembered the first time you ate me out and I thought I'd never stop coming. And while I was remembering, my pussy was just getting so juicy."

Damn it! There was too much steam in the room! I was hard as a rock just from imagining what happened as I listened to Rita tell her story. Here she was, just a few feet away from me and I knew what she was doing. I stroked my cock in time with her breathing, wishing I could see what was going on. Then she turned the water off. Rita and I weren't five feet away from each other and as the water died, the steam began to slowly dissipate.

"Don't move," she whispered. "Every so often, the steam jets detect the temperature is too high or the moisture in the room is at max and they shut off. I was lying back against the wall with my eyes closed, just caught up in my dream and stroking my clit like I'm doing now. Are you stroking your cock, Doc? Doesn't the steamy room just take you off to a dream world?"

I was, indeed, stroking my cock as I sat with my left foot up on the bench and, as it relaxed and slid outward, I encountered Rita's right foot. For a moment, we sat, silently stroking ourselves with just our toes touching.

"When the steam shut off, the room gradually began to clear, just like ours is doing," she whispered. Without the noise of the running water, her voice seemed to come from everywhere in the room. I opened my eyes and could see her through the thinning fog, her hand still buried between her thighs. Her breasts rose and fell rapidly. I could feel the pre-come leaking from my cock as I smeared it across the head and down the shaft.

"I thought I heard a noise and opened my eyes," Rita continued. "Directly opposite me, I saw Gabriella, like a mirror image, sitting against the opposite corner with a dreamy look on her face, stroking her clit. She opened her eyes and saw me. I thought for a moment that one of us was going to bolt from the room, but neither of us moved. I could see her eyes flick down to my pussy, just as I boldly looked right at hers. Oh, God! It was beautiful. Gabriella has black hair. It's cut short; I guess so it's easier to put up under her helmet when she rides outside. She doesn't have an ounce of fat on her body. Her breasts are barely bumps on her chest—two raisins on a breadboard. But she's no little girl. Muscles ripple all down her body, right to the small patch of black hair just above her slit. She isn't overbuilt. She has a hard flat tummy, but when you get to her slit, your eyes are drawn down to her incredible thighs and calves. I've seen biker's calves that look all hard and stringy, but Gabriella's calves are beautifully shaped. She's thin and lean, but incredibly beautiful. She's the kind of girl you could paint and see every muscle beneath her taut skin.

"And we just stayed there like that, looking at each other while we stroked our pussies."

I could see Rita's fingers strumming away at her clit and I knew I wasn't going to last long as I stroked my cock. It was a beautiful image. She reached up and turned the water back on. The steam began to rise again.

"When the steam lowered enough, the jets kicked in again. All that time we never changed our positions. It was like I could feel her fingering her pussy just like I was doing to my own. She was getting closer and I knew we were both going to go off soon. I could feel it building in me while she was displaying herself to me and I was showing her everything I've got. As the steam in the room built up, I lost sight of her again."

The steam in our shower was building up as well and I was sure Rita was timing her story to the visual effect of the water.

"The last thing I saw, Gabriella was panting and throwing her head back with her mouth open." I could no longer see Rita but the image burned in my mind had me on a hair trigger. One more stroke…

"Ahhhh!" Rita moaned from out of the steam cloud. She was answered by my own groan of pleasure as I went off as well. I collapsed against the corner of the shower with my semen spattered all around and on me. I would be surprised if I hadn't shot some all the way over to where Rita was sitting. I was panting and out of breath. We just let the water splash down and increase the steam.

"When I'd caught my breath, I ran out of the steam room, grabbed my clothes and bolted for my car. I didn't bother to put on underwear. I barely got my skirt and blouse on before I was out the door and driving here." Rita's voice had shifted. It was no longer across from me, but over to my right. I started to move.

"You should paint now," she whispered. I heard the door to the bathroom close. When I'd rinsed my body and turned the showers off, she was gone.

I went to the studio.

# 13
# Enticement

IT WAS MY fifth piece from the new me. It had taken three days because I had to sleep sometime. I was worried about laying down my brushes for fear I wouldn't be able to pick up the vision again, but when I woke up, it was fresh in my mind.

It was a good thing I had four rookies to pass my work to. I paid no attention to my job all week. When I checked in at the office, they were all excited about the showings they had scheduled. They were still working through the list of leads they'd acquired from the Morrison open houses. It was mid-January and people were still getting over the holiday rush.

Friday night, Rita arrived at my door with kisses and love. I took her straight to the studio. There was my painting.

It was bigger than anything I'd ever painted—a full four feet high and six wide. I'd had to start by building an easel I could set it on. The canvas was washed with gray. Only a few strokes defined the figures leaning against the opposite edges. Their outstretched feet melted into each other behind the billowing steam. The figure on the right was a dirty blonde, her hair wet and plastered against her face. She was voluptuous. Her face was cast down to her left with a look of ecstasy. The rictus of her orgasm peeked through the steam. Beads of sweat dripped from her brow.

The figure on the left was thinner and leaned out of the picture with her short dark hair also plastered against the side of her face. Her head was thrown back as she howled toward the sky. In the foreground, their legs extended off canvas into the depth of the fog. One hand of each figure was dropped into their laps, pussies barely visible through the steam. The other hand was stretched toward its mirror image, not quite touching.

Rita stood looking at the painting for a long time with a smile playing on her lips. "You do love me," she whispered at last. I wrapped my arms around her and she melted into them, lifting her lips to me. I kissed them with gentle passion. When our mouths parted, she heaved a deep sigh. "You need to have a showing."

⸻ ꩜ ⸻

FIRST, HOWEVER, I needed to show my lover how much I cared for her. We didn't go out often, as strange as that seemed. Often on Friday evening, I would cook a special dinner and we would watch a movie on television, eventually leading us to bed and lovemaking.

I determined, however, that this special painting deserved a special evening celebration. I didn't want to risk driving when I might be drinking so called Uber to take us to the restaurant where I'd made dinner reservations. The Union Broiler had two locations. The one in the suburbs was at the top of an office building and looked out across the city to the mountains in the distance. People who could afford their prices went after a hard day of work in business suits and dresses. They looked out at the expansive view and drank cocktails with cute names while they awaited their food.

The location downtown was built on a pier that extended over the lapping waters of a lake where boats tied up and discharged diners. The food was the same, the price was the same, but the clientele tended to be more insouciant and affable than the suburban location. I'd donned a jacket and Rita wore a dress, but neither were what we'd wear to someplace 'fancy.'

Still, we ordered cocktails and appetizers and settled in for a long dining experience. We enjoyed crab cakes followed by a Caesar salad, filet mignon, and a dessert called 'chocolate decadence.' It was all enjoyed with a bottle of local merlot.

"Why such a fancy celebration for this work of art?" she asked. "I'm loving every morsel and every sip, but why so extravagant?"

Before I could answer, our very attentive waitress came to our table with a refill for our water and to take away the appetizer plates. We sat mostly parallel to the windows but I noticed she stayed beside Rita and leaned across the table to remove my dishes. It was only momentary, but I saw a flash of creamy white skin as her scoop neck blouse fell loosely from her throat revealing the generous mounds of her breasts. Then she was gone. My distracted eyes followed her shapely ass as she returned to the kitchen.

"Doc?" Rita said. "Where did you go?"

"Um… Spelunking, I guess. I just caught sight of a canyon I was tempted to climb into."

"Ah. She does have a rather nice valley between the mountains. Should I go? Perhaps if we had a bit of a tiff, she would try to comfort you," Rita giggled.

"No, no! I'm truly sorry to have been distracted. The display was rather pointed," I said.

"Yes? A point on each peak?"

"It makes no difference. I'm sure it was accidental and she'd be terribly embarrassed that we… or I noticed. About the extravagance. Yes. Well, I'm beginning to feel more at home with my new style. When you think about it, the painting of Allison that started this was months ago. It was three months after that when you brought Kelly to play with us. The next three paintings were done in the two months since Thanksgiving. It's becoming hard to take a portrait commission when I know I can paint something far more dramatic. I think this celebration is of the rebirth of my art and is an honor to the woman who made it happen."

I raised my glass to Rita and we touched just as our waitress returned to remove our bread and salad plates with the entrée soon to follow. Once again, she stayed near Rita's shoulder as she reached across the table to take my plate and then again with a brush and tabletop dustpan. The motion of sweeping the breadcrumbs from the tablecloth set her breasts swaying in a delightful way. Then she set our entrées in front of us and poured more wine. I was certain now that she was intentionally facing me specifically to give me the view. There was really no other reason.

"Hurry," Rita whispered. "We need to eat and talk between the distractions."

"That was highly unexpected."

"She must get tipped a lot."

"I'll remember that. But my point was that I think I am making a true transition in my painting. And I wanted to mark that with an elegant meal and the woman I love."

"Doc, that is why I think you need a showing."

"My love, it isn't really that easy. I've only five of the pieces so far. Even a modest show would require a dozen. And the space needed. I've indulged myself in larger canvases and few galleries have the space to show them. I'm not disagreeing that I need a showing. Just that it will take quite a long time to arrange one and to paint enough canvases to make it worthwhile. To either myself or a gallery owner."

"I wasn't suggesting it should be next weekend. I see the same issues you do. That's why an event like this needs to be planned months out. Perhaps more than a year. And my dear artist, even though you have a new and addictive style, there is nothing wrong with your paintings up to this time. You are still one of the most prized portrait artists in the city."

"How do you figure that? I paint pretty pictures of wealthy ladies, but that is not a big business either. And besides, those paintings are commissioned. They are bought and paid for before I put brush to paint."

"I read something," she said. "I caught just a note in Home Spectacular this month. Certainly, you read it, don't you?"

"I usually glance through the copy that comes to the office but I don't think I've seen this month's issue."

"I'm surprised no one mentioned it to you," she said. "They did an article on the Brainerd home. A tour conducted by Mrs. Brainerd. In one of the photos, they showed a portrait captioned, 'Louise Brainerd as painted by the area's premier portrait artist, DR Peters.' Not a big mention, but high praise."

"Dear me! I had no idea. I did that painting… It must have been ten years ago."

"Well, it still hangs in a place of prominence in their home. It's weathered the years better than she has."

"Still, most of my portraits are owned by the clients. There wouldn't be any of them to show. And certainly none to sell."

"I'm going to investigate on your behalf, Doc. I promise not to make any arrangements, but just to learn about what it takes. You need to market your ability."

"Funny, isn't it. I can go into super sales mode and market the hell out of a home but find I'm falling over myself when I think about marketing my paintings."

Our waitress returned to remove our plates and then returned again with dessert and again with coffee. Each time she approached the table she flashed me a glorious view of her tits. The last time, I glanced up from the display and found her looking directly at my eyes. *Caught!* She blushed slightly but smiled and stayed bent over another few seconds before leaving and returning with our check.

'Thank you, Lori' was scrawled across the bottom of the bill. I looked for a phone number but she hadn't gone that far.

"Speaking of marketing, do you have a business card for your art and portrait business?" Rita asked.

"Oh, yes. Seldom used. I seem to hand out a lot of real estate business cards."

"Leave one of your art cards with the tip. Then hand both to me. She should see that I'm the one inviting her contact." Rita quickly wrote her name and number on my card and we left. It was a lovely and inspiring dinner.

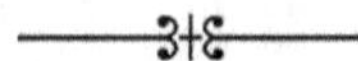

"THINK OF WHAT fun you could have playing on and between those peaks," Rita whispered as we kissed and fondled in bed.

"I'm quite satisfied with the peaks in my hands," I said. I scooted down so I could pay oral attention to her nipples as well as fondling her breasts.

"Of course. But while you were looking down the blouse, I had ample opportunity to appreciate the derriere near at hand. I would say she is an example of something fresh and interested."

"But why would she do that?" I protested. "It's not like I am a particularly handsome man. And it was obvious that I was enrapt in my companion except when she leaned between us. What possible gain could she have from displaying herself to me?"

"In addition to the generous tip you left? Hmm. I'm not sure. It just didn't look that mercenary to me. I managed to watch her out the corner of my eye and she didn't seem to be flirting with other customers. At least not with the same technique. I think there is a story there. And very likely a new painting."

"I love you, Rita. I am happy with what I have in my bed and would welcome you far more often."

"Let me welcome you then, dear. Welcome between my legs. Oh, yes. Press into me. Whether in your studio or in your bed, we are partners."

I moved into Rita smoothly and rocked back and forth as we both built up steam to our orgasms. This. If I could only capture this feeling on canvas, I would know I was successful. This feeling that began in my cock and extended up my spine. I could feel her in the core of my being as I thrust into her core. And my lovely assistant Rita called out her climax coaxing my own along with her.

I ONLY HEARD one side of the phone conversation Rita had on Saturday afternoon. I'd begun to take a serious look through the paintings I had in storage to see if any had the quality I would need for an exhibition. Or if any sparked a flame that I could fan into a new piece in my newer style. I was also playing through the slides of my paintings. I was looking for the portrait of Mrs. Brainerd.

"This is Rita. — Oh, hello. I hoped you'd call. I'm Doc Peters' assistant. — Yes, we are always looking for models. Would you like to try? — When Doc is in an artistic zone, he is very focused and sometimes works around the clock. Models are not required to put in those hours. You will be paid for an eight-hour work day, most of which you will be nude. If you decide to spend more than the eight hours, it is personal time.— $500 for a full day.— Why don't we meet for an interview tomorrow at noon? Let's say at Red Robin. We'll have lunch and if everything works out, set a time for posing that would be convenient for both of you. — Thank you for calling. Good day."

I stood looking at my lovely assistant with my mouth open. Since when did I hire models? And who were we interviewing at lunch Sunday? Rita sat staring at her phone.

"That was interesting," Rita said.

"What was it all about? I haven't hired a model in a very long time. Do you think I'm made of money? $500 a day? Rita, what is going on?"

"That was our waitress from last night," she grinned. "Her name is Lori Kraft. She responded to my number on the back of your card."

"It seems a little sudden," I said. "There was nothing in her flirtation last night that indicated she wanted to model. She didn't even know I was an artist at the time. It was more an exhibitionist kind of thing."

"Yes. That's why I didn't just invite her over now. The interview will be a way to suss out what her real motivation is. But wouldn't you like to see those mountains on display again? Totally unconcealed? I can tell you from my perspective, the ass was fine. You need to do some experimental drawings. Allow your creative spirit to take flight before you have an idea of where it will take you."

"Have you become my psychologist now?"

"Doc, honey. I'm your lover and your research assistant. I'm studying and observing the kind of encounter and the resulting painting to see if there is a repeatable pattern. If nothing sparks the new and unusual from your encounter with Lori, you can at least do a portrait of a young woman and have an example of your portraiture to exhibit."

"Yes, I suppose there is that. I would still like to know what inspired her exhibitionist display." I looked at the image on screen of a painting I'd done several years ago. Something about it said 'fresh,' unlike some of my stale paintings. "What do you think of this one?"

⎯⎯⎯ ❀ ⎯⎯⎯

Lunch with Lori Kraft was enlightening. I had the opportunity this time to truly assess the woman without being utterly distracted by her boobs. Not that she'd done anything to prevent me from being distracted at our interview. She was nearly six feet tall, something I'd been unable to guess at the Union Broiler. Her hair was medium brown with eyes that matched. Her generous breasts were unfettered and the low-cut blouse she wore did little to conceal them. She also wore a short, tight skirt and high heels that showed off very sexy legs.

"Please order what you'd like, Lori," I said. "It's not often Rita and I get to interview someone. I don't exactly advertise."

"Thank you. I'll have the Southwestern Salad. Tea to drink."

Rita also had a salad and a soft drink. I'm afraid I indulged a craving for a burger and accompanied it with a beer.

"Excuse the rudeness of my question, but before we talk about art and posing, I need to confirm your age," Rita said. "How old are you?"

"I'm twenty-two, a student at the University and studying Sociology. I also play varsity volleyball which cuts into my work time."

"Have you done any modeling work before?" I asked.

"Well, sort of. I got caught up in a scam and there are a few nude photos of me floating around online. I figure posing for a painting won't result in the same kind of exposure," Lori said. Our lunches arrived and we just chit-chatted a bit around our full mouths.

"I have to ask, Lori: What inspired the flirtatious display on Friday night? Was that how you treat all customers?" I was pretty sure it wasn't, since I hadn't noticed her in that posture at any other tables.

"Um… No. I… uh… It was a task my mistress gave me." She blushed brightly.

"Your mistress?" Rita asked.

"Yes, ma'am. I'll do anything for her."

"And she told you to flirt with Doc?"

"Not exactly. She said to pick out one man during the evening and flash him. Once I got started, I sort of couldn't stop. I guess that's why she gave me the task."

"And what did she say about calling us and posing?" I asked.

"Sometimes my mistress gives me difficult tasks. This is an example. She said I had to decide for myself if I would contact you. I decided after I looked up your information online. You paint nice pictures."

"Most of the time. Sometimes they aren't nice at all," I said.

"Doc, what you call not nice are extremely powerful and important," Rita said. She turned to Lori. "He's quite humble. I'm looking for a subject he can go a step beyond portraiture with. I like you, but he makes the decision."

"I understand."

"Do you want to pose for me?" I asked.

She hesitated a minute. "Yes, sir. I do."

"Do you understand the bulk of your posing will be nude? Props and drapes, but nothing else."

"Yes, sir. I understand." I could see her cheeks flush again.

"Does that embarrass you?" I asked.

"Um… No, sir. It excites me." Hmm. That was interesting. I cocked an eyebrow at Rita and she nodded.

"Do you understand that there will be times when I need to touch you? To position you correctly? To get the pose I want?"

"Ohh! Tha… That's okay, I guess. You can treat me like one of those little art dolls they sell. The ones that have joints and you bend into any position."

"Mannequins," I supplied.

"Yes."

———— ❧ ————

WE AGREED TO start Monday morning at ten. I took Rita home and we spent the remainder of Sunday in bed. Rita wanted to play with one of my mannequins, experimenting with what positions they could be put in. I didn't think a human body could actually achieve some of her contortions. A few were obscene, even by my standards. Rita tried several of the poses in our bed and I attempted entry in each one.

One thing there was no question about was wanting to paint Lori's breasts. I would want a good picture of the enticement I'd seen in the restaurant. However, it was rare for artists to try to capture the female form from that angle. Few pictures have a woman with her boobs displayed hanging down as she bends over. I wanted to capture that pose—leaning over our table—in various stages of undress. Rita agreed.

"But you'll want an image that is more laid back as well," she said. "I mean, reclining. Submissive. I can see playing with Lori several times."

"Playing with her?"

"Positioning her to model, of course. You would want to get her in the right position, wouldn't you?" She sounded so innocent when she said that, but the pose she adopted, crawling up my body as I lay back with my cock vanishing between her tits, was inspirational.

Rita decided to take a couple of days off work just as I was, to make sure Lori felt comfortable. From our playtime, I'd say Rita just wanted to help put Lori in position.

———— ❧ ————

I HAD MY café table setting ready in the studio when Lori arrived Monday morning. Rita greeted her and served her coffee and a sweet roll while I puttered in the studio. At ten o'clock, she led my new model into the studio. Lori was dressed just as she had been Friday night in a short tight skirt and the scoop neck blouse that would fall away from her tits when she bent over. I decided to begin there. I think she was surprised I didn't want her to strip straight away.

I did a few warm-up sketches of her as a serving girl and then had her lean over the table as she had when she served me. Yes, there were those snowy breasts capped with taut nipples. For the first time, I physically positioned her. I seated myself at the table as if she were serving me—or teasing me—and reached out to adjust her shoulders slightly. I moved one arm so it didn't trap her blouse against her breast. She was cooperative but caught her breath when I touched her blouse to loosen it slightly from her shoulders and make it obvious I was looking at her boobs. She didn't move, though.

I returned to my easel and repositioned it so I had the same view as if I were sitting at the table. I sketched the scene.

"How about this?" Rita asked when I'd finished the sketch. She'd dressed in a similar manner but a bit more refined. It was obvious she would be playing the customer in this scene. She sat at the café table and held a menu card. She had Lori lean over her to point something out on the menu. Of course, from the other side of the table, I had a beautiful view of Lori's breast.

I made adjustments to the pose, freely touching both women to get them in the right position. I moved Lori's blouse off her shoulder and scooped her breast out by sliding my hand down across her left tit. She shuddered but made no effort to escape my caress. Rita smiled at me. I could see her own nipples poking at her nearly transparent blouse. I started sketching.

And so the day went, the poses including less clothing and the touches being more prolonged. The final pose of the day had Lori lying back across the table with her tits pointing to the sky and just at the height of Rita's lips. She looked like dessert and when Rita's tongue snaked out to touch Lori's nipple, I think they may both have come.

"The big clock on the wall says we have completed our giornata."
"What is that?"
"A day's work in artist speak," I laughed. "It means it's Miller time."
"Oh. I don't drink beer."

"Neither does he," Rita laughed. "Would you join us for a glass of wine?"

"Oh! Thank you. That would be nice." She stood and stretched. She was truly stacked. But for such huge breasts, they didn't sag much nor collapse significantly when she was on her back. I'd thought at first, they must be fake, but I'd managed a few good squeezes during the day and they certainly felt soft and pliable enough. I appreciated the view as Rita joined her in stretching. Rita still had her panties on. Lori was completely nude, even though I'd only ever sketched her torso. She glanced over to where her clothes were neatly folded and then looked at Rita.

"There's really no reason to get dressed for wine or dinner," Rita said. "Let's go relax in the living room while Doc pours us our wine." Lori lit up at the thought of being naked in the house when she wasn't working. She hid her smile and bowed her head in acquiescence. Rita led her to the living room and I followed the two round asses, thoroughly enjoying the view.

14

## Pin-up Girl

I HAVE FOUND MYSELF in stranger circumstances. Not often. I poured wine for the two naked women in my living room and felt highly over-dressed. They were quite different to look at. Rita is nicely shaped, breasts that I loved to play, and light brown hair that frames a pixie-ish face. Lori was about the same height as Rita, with lighter, almost honey blonde hair. And her large breasts seemed to beg for attention. Any man and many women would love to play with them.

"Vargas," I said out of the blue.

"What?"

"Is that another art term like the giorno?"

"Giornata," I corrected Lori. "In a manner of speaking, yes. Alberto Vargas was an artist who specialized in pin-up girls in the forties through the sixties. He made the World War II pin-up girls famous after having served as the artist for the Ziegfeld Follies and several Hollywood movies. He later worked for *Esquire* magazine and for *Playboy* magazine. Did literally hundreds of paintings of women over the course of three-plus decades."

"And what brings up this ancient artist?" Rita giggled.

"Ah. He was known for pictures of nude and nearly nude or highly suggestive poses of women. One of the things that seemed to be a mark of his paintings were that they were all generously endowed with gravity-defying breasts. Much like Lori's," I said. I didn't think her

123

nipples could get any harder, but the points stiffened and her areolae puffed a bit. She had just a bit of a blush.

"Oh, yes," Rita said, shifting so she could stroke one of Lori's breasts. "Did you notice that when she did the pose lying back on the table that they hardly flattened at all? They are so full yet firm. And these nipples are utterly succulent." Rita punctuated her comments by leaning in to gently suck on Lori's nipple. The young woman sucked in her breath and captured Rita's head with her hand to hold her against her breast.

My immediate take-away was that Lori liked being objectified. She liked being talked about as if she were not a part of the conversation. I moved from my seat in the chair opposite the women to perch on the arm of the sofa next to Lori.

"What I want to do, truly, is to capture the beauty of these breasts on the canvas." I stroked down her shoulder and over her unoccupied breast, holding and gently squeezing it. "We are so fortunate to have found a real Vargas Girl model. Of course, it was not only about the models' breasts. They each had faces that were fresh, innocent, playful, and sometimes mischievous. With lips that were very kissable." I leaned forward and pressed my lips to Lori's. Her eyes flashed open in surprise and then she relaxed and poured herself into the kiss.

Rita and I both pulled back from Lori at the same time. She looked very disappointed. "What else?" she whispered. Rita smiled at me.

"If the pin-up was exposed, it often looked accidental. A gust of wind blew up her skirt. A blouse accidentally slipped to show more than intended. The model looked surprised and slightly embarrassed for the slip, but made no move to correct it." I began moving Lori's arms, much as if she were a mannequin. Rita quickly saw what I was doing and joined in the posing. It was a lot like I'd done with her the first time I posed her. "Usually, the pin-up was a full-length image. So, of course, it was important that she have a perfect waist, hips, and legs," I said, moving down her body to position her limbs so as to emphasize their shape. I noticed Rita's panties had sometime disappeared and she was quite boldly sliding her pussy down one of Lori's thighs, leaving a shiny wet streak.

"Doc, do you suppose Vargas slept with all his models?" Rita asked. Lori shivered and caught her breath as my hand glided over her mons. Her legs parted slightly.

"I believe everyone who saw one of his paintings thought, 'There's a lucky guy who had sex with her.' I understand, however, that Vargas was also happily married and when his wife died in, I believe, '74, he was so bereaved that he quit painting entirely. He died in the mid-80s."

"How sad. I'm sure it was simply because his wife was his partner and joined in his escapades with the models," Rita said. "After all, how could a man or woman resist making love to such a compliant sex object. Her juices are running freely. Don't you think we should take her to bed?"

I looked at Lori. Her eyes had taken on a pleading look and she nodded slightly. I smiled.

"Let's see what kind of positions we can put the model in when we reach our bed," I said. I collected Lori in my arms and guided her to the bedroom. Rita gathered up our glasses and the wine bottle to bring them along. Lori moved almost as if spell-bound, willing to assume any of the positions we could come up with.

⁓ 3†8 ⁓

It was a short night as far as sleep went. The more outlandish the position was in which I fucked Lori, the more enthusiastic she became. Even Rita was exhausted by the time we finally collapsed to sleep. When I woke up, Lori was nursing on my cock like it was a baby's pacifier. When she saw I was awake, she redoubled her efforts until I spurted weakly into her mouth. She showed the meagre offering and then dove between Rita's legs and attempted to cram it into her vagina with her tongue.

I crawled out of bed and made coffee, leaving the pot in the kitchen for the girls as I took a mug to the studio. I was sure that if I tried to take them coffee in the bedroom, I wouldn't get to the studio for the rest of the day.

And I had something to paint. I already knew the painting of Lori leaning over the table to show me her boobs would be one painting. But I'd also seen something in our playtime last night that I wanted to capture.

"Now lie back and let us pleasure you," I'd said. "Good slaves take their rewards as well as their punishments."

The instant look of submission that washed over her face was a sight to behold. She had flopped back on the bed with a look that said, "I am yours. Take me wherever you wish." Rita and I had spent half an hour tag-teaming her until she'd cried out multiple orgasms. Then we had dinner. It was nearly ten pm.

But that look… That demeanor of absolute submission… I don't think I'd ever seen anything like it before. When I looked at the other paintings I'd done so far, I realized they were all of women in control. They were women getting exactly what they wanted.

I sketched several scenes from memory, trying to find the right pose for her so I could do a polished drawing. The more I sketched, the more I realized that Lori, too, had been in control. She was getting exactly what she wanted.

Rita brought me a plate of eggs and toast with a fresh mug of coffee. As I ate, she glanced through my morning sketches and nodded.

"I may have to eat her to orgasm in order to get that look again, but I see where you are coming from," she said. "I've heard it called 'topping from the bottom.' She got exactly what she wanted by being totally submissive. Ignore her when she comes down. Just be ready to draw. I'll take care of posing her." I nodded my agreement and finished breakfast.

When they both entered the studio a while later, I was sitting on my stool with a drawing pad on my easel. Lori started to approach but Rita directed her away from looking at anything I was doing.

"This is just like last night," Rita told her. "I'll be placing you in the positions we want to fuck you in. Only this time, instead of fucking you, Doc will be drawing. You'll need to hold your pose until he's finished his sketch and tells me I can move you to the next pose." They moved the daybed to my posing platform and Rita had Lori simply sprawl back on the bed. She adjusted a few things, more for the opportunity of moving Lori and letting her know who was in control than to improve the pose.

I sketched.

Rita posed Lori again.

I sketched.

By noon, we had half a dozen poses captured but I'd not managed that one that I wanted.

"Let's break for lunch," I said. "Refresh yourselves. I need to look at the setting." Rita shot me a curious look, but led Lori upstairs and began preparing a light lunch. I looked through my morning's sketches and then at the sketches before she came down to pose, trying to figure out what I was missing. It was quickly obvious.

I have models pose on a low platform—a kind of stage, if you will. It helps to instill a feeling of detachment in the model. She, too, is an artist, performing on stage. But as a result, a model lying fully reclined on the day bed is just slightly below eye-level. The perspective was entirely wrong for what I wanted to achieve.

When I'd conceived of the idea, I'd been descending on her luscious body to fuck her. My perspective was well above when I saw that look of satisfaction in her eye.

I quickly moved the day bed down to the floor level and switched my stool and easel to the stage. That was better, but still not right. I went to the garage and retrieved a six-foot step ladder. It wouldn't be comfortable, but the view from this height—sitting on the top step— was what I needed. I replaced the easel with my portable sketch pad board and tested balancing on the ladder. My head was just touching the ten-foot ceiling, but I could maintain the position for a while. I had a bird's eye view.

———— ⊰⊱ ————

LORI GLANCED AT me when she returned to the studio, but Rita immediately directed her to the bed and started posing her.

"You know how to look turned on?" Rita asked.

"Um…" Lori kind of grimaced and shrugged her shoulders.

"Well, you must look turned on for this pose. Lie back and let me work on you." Lori lay back, looking up at me. When Rita began diddling the girl's clit, Lori sat up to look.

"Don't move!" I snapped. It was the first thing I'd said to the girl all day. She was so shocked she flopped back in her original position, staring at me. I quickly sketched the pose and turned the page. As soon as Rita heard me turn to a new page, she moved to pose Lori anew.

"What would be the best way for you to offer yourself to him?" Rita said. "Look at him up there like God gazing down on your helpless body. What will he do with it? How will he take his pleasure from you? Will he pinch your proud nipples to make them stand up straight? Will he suck on them? Will he move behind you and press his rod into your wet slit? How will you welcome him when you are frozen in place?"

As Rita continued her narration, moving Lori to a position lying three-quarters on her side, she touched the model freely, bending to suck a nipple and leave a trail of saliva running down the boob. She stroked Lori's side and hips, ultimately thrusting a finger into her depth. Lori gasped and her eyes began to get glassy as she was overcome by lust. But she stayed still, not moving from one position until I turned to a new page and Rita positioned her again. It was nearly six o'clock when I closed my sketchbook and started down the ladder. Lori still hadn't moved and Rita was still plunging a finger wetly into her vagina.

"I think we have punished our slave enough for today," I said. Lori moaned as Rita withdrew from her.

"Please," she whimpered.

I began removing my clothes and Rita stood to help me. She removed what remained of her own clothes as well.

"A good slave must receive her rewards as well as she does her punishments," I repeated from the night before. "Now lie back and let us pleasure you." Lori's face got that look of complete satisfaction that I'd noted the night before. She lay back and opened herself to our ministrations. This time, instead of simply teasing her and bringing her to orgasm, Rita rose and straddled her face as I notched my cock into her dripping pussy. Lori moaned and instantly began humping back at me as she vigorously worked her tongue on Rita's clit.

It was not an overwhelmingly long bout of sex. Rita and I kissed over the top of the girl and I plunged my rod in and held it there as a stream of semen jetted forth. Rita, too, lit off when Lori clenched up and moaned her orgasm. We were all quite satisfied.

"Shall we celebrate the end of the giornata with a glass of wine?" Rita asked.

"I must hurry home now," Lori said. "My mistress will want to hear about my adventure. I need to get to her."

"Ah, yes. Of course. Please give your mistress our greetings and our thanks," I said. I'd stopped at the ATM Sunday afternoon and reached in my wallet for ten $100-bills. When Lori was dressed, I handed them to her.

"Thank you, sir. Thank you, ma'am. This is an experience I will never forget." We kissed her goodbye and she was off.

❈

"Are you going to paint now?" Rita asked as we finished a light meal. We'd not been back in the studio after Lori left, choosing to have a quiet glass of wine and a simple dinner.

"No. I don't dare right now," I said. "I need to go to the office and start filling my pipeline for spring listings. I can't just take weeks off of my job. I'd soon be working at McDonald's. And you shouldn't take more time off, either. We won't have any vacation time left to actually go on vacation!"

"Yes. My head knows what you are saying is right. My heart wants to fling it all away and just work on promoting your art and lining up tasty models for you to devour," Rita laughed.

"I never did that before I met you," I said. "At least, not often."

"I'm not complaining. I've had more excitement and adventure in the past year than the rest of my life. I am, however, going to record another data point. How long do you think you'll need to wait before you start painting?"

"I don't have any open houses this weekend. I could start Friday night and work through Monday. There are two paintings to be done of Lori. Maybe, eventually, even more. My alternative is to begin tomorrow night after work and discipline myself to set aside my paints after four or five hours and go to bed. At least the idea would be fresh when I start."

"On the other hand, you don't like to interrupt a painting like that. Do you think you can maintain the creative flow well enough when it is interrupted?"

"There's only one way to find out, I guess. I'll start tomorrow night and if it proves too difficult, I'll just wait until Friday to get a fresh start."

"If you aren't going to start painting tonight, I'll stay and keep you company. After a session like the past two days, I find I want to be held and reassured by you," she said. "Do you find that strange? I think of myself as independent and capable. I don't feel insecure. I'm confident in my work, both at the lab and when I'm making phone calls about your art. But when there is a lull in our busy lives, I just want to be held by you. I want your artist's soul to reassure me that I'm loved. It's very unscientific."

I didn't really have a response for her, other than to take her to bed and hold her. She was a treasure.

———— ❊ ————

PREPPING THE CANVAS was close to a four-hour job the way I approached it. Rather than just choosing one of the poses and developing it, I decided to work on both poses at the same time. They were significantly different, even in the size of canvas I used. The pose of Lori leaning over the table was a small painting, about two feet square.

I chose a three-by-five canvas for the bed scene and decided to orient it vertically.

Once I had the canvases chosen and ready to work, I started sketching, moving back and forth between the two. I would call the square piece my tribute to Vargas, focusing only on the model. The table and background would only be suggested. The important bit of the painting would be the emphasis on Lori's exposed nipples and breasts. The larger piece would have more detail in the rumpled bedding with a blanket casually tossed across her so her pussy was not quite exposed. It would be hinted at. After I laid in that detail, I returned to the smaller canvas and focused on her eyes and lips, noting how her expression would drag the viewer's eyes into her exposed cleavage.

I wasn't quite finished with the sketches, but when my alarm beeped at midnight, I dutifully put away my supplies and retired to bed. Stopping before I started applying paint to the canvases was good.

———❃———

Thursday evening, I returned to my studio at four in the afternoon. I was too antsy to focus at the office and one more call to an uninterested homeowner was more than I could face. I fixed sandwiches and soft drinks to take to the studio with me. I knew once I started painting, I wouldn't want to interrupt the process to eat unless the food was right at hand.

I finished the details in the sketches and chose my background colors. The two paintings would have a similar palette, but the larger would be far less controlled in the illustrative quality of the portraiture. I was not going to get the same effects as Vargas. I didn't use an airbrush, which was how he achieved such delicate curvature in his models. However, there were other ways to achieve these effects. I used washes and gentle blending with less contrast in my colors.

On the other hand, the large painting of Lori on the bed jumped off the canvas in its dimensionality. I layered thick textures with a palette knife and then thinned the same paint to apply with a delicate brush in the small painting.

It was a pain to quit at midnight when my alarm beeped.

———❧———

FRIDAY, MY ROOKIES and I did a tour of several newer listings and discussed which of our contacts we might match up with them. We'd have a lot of work to do the next week if we followed through on all the ideas we'd generated. After the tour, we all went back to the office and I slipped out early to get back to my painting.

All restraints were off as I approached the canvases Friday evening. I continued to move fluidly between the two paintings, both of which were shaping up nicely. When I was too tired to continue painting, I simply stretched out on the daybed for a few hours and then returned to my paints. Somewhere along the line, breakfast and coffee appeared for me. Rita must have been here. I couldn't hear her moving in the house, though.

I continued my focused painting around the clock, sleeping on the daybed when I was too tired to paint and eating food when it was placed near me. Rita didn't say a word the entire time. Or at least she never said anything I heard.

Monday morning, I'd slowed down as I examined each painting for missing details. I thought of what it had been like with Lori in the studio. In my mind, I lifted away the folds of fabric that concealed her most intimate treasures and felt myself sinking into her hot pussy. She had been perfectly submissive the entire two days she was with us. And she got the perfect satisfaction of what she wanted. I sat back and decided to title the two pieces *Enticement* and *Submission*.

I took a long hot shower and went to bed.

15

## From the Past

I HAD SEVEN PAINTINGS I'd completed since my new artistic awakening. It was almost like being newly out of art school and thinking I could paint masterpieces. But I had precious few as evidence. In the meantime, I needed to earn a living and that meant selling real estate. It pretty much pre-empted everything else. Even my weekends with Rita seemed rushed as I started scheduling open houses for the early spring market.

I focused on high-end properties that often took a year or more to move. My sales record told a story of much faster than average turnaround. I focused on the personal touch when dealing with this clientele. When they reached the level of income needed to purchase one of these houses, they were typically in it for the long haul. They would be in that house for ten to twenty years or more. Everything needed to be perfect.

I started my campaign with Holly Park. Most of the homes in the exclusive neighborhood in which my team had sold the Morrison house, were million-dollar properties. I had excellent referrals from both the Morrisons and the Cartwrights, who had purchased the home. Now, I sent personal letters to the owners of each home in the community.

There is a 'trick' to sending these letters. One that my rookies needed to learn. The letters needed to be perfect. The method taught in real estate school is to put together a marketing letter and send it to everyone. This clientele could tell that approach a mile away. Those letters were likely to be tossed in recycling without ever entering the house. The letters were also rife with spelling and grammar errors. When I received mail with my name misspelled on the envelope, I didn't bother to open it. And inside, the letter should represent the meticulous care I would take in marketing and selling the home.

A personal letter, but not informal. I didn't hand address plain white envelopes. Nor would I use a window envelope. That just screamed mass mailing. I had linen stationery with raised type return address and inside address on the letterhead. It was just slightly off-white but not so much so that it stuck out like a sore thumb. Subtlety was the key.

In the era of personal computers and word processing, there was really no excuse for misspelled or poorly formatted letters. My letters were immaculate. I carefully watched for homonyms, making especially sure that I corrected were/we're/where, then/than, your/you're, their/there/they're. And if there was any doubt at all regarding the spelling of a word or a company name, I looked it up.

My letters were signed with a fountain pen and left to dry thoroughly before they were folded. They were never more than one page. They always included a personal touch, with family names when possible. For example:

> *Dear Mr. and Mrs. Stackhouse,*
>
> *Spring is just around the corner and I note that your son, John Jr., will be ready for middle school in the fall. Congratulations on raising such a fine young man.*
>
> *This might be the ideal time for you to consider a new home. You've been at 473 Lilac Lane since before John Jr.'s birth. At the time you purchased this home, your needs were much different than they are now. You might be thinking of moving to a home more suited to entertaining and more convenient to John's middle school.*
>
> *The market is also turning. This means it is a good time to get an offer in on a home before prices resume their upward trend, and a good time to prepare your current home for sale as soon as*

*school is out. The summer market will be strong this year and I believe we can get top dollar for your present home.*

*I'd like to discuss the possibilities with you in person. I will plan to call you Monday evening the 18th at 7:00 p.m. If this is inconvenient for you, please feel free to call or text me at 555-555-5555 and I will arrange my schedule to suit yours.*

*Thank you for hearing me out on this. I look forward to talking to you in person.*

*Sincerely,*
*D.R. 'Doc' Peters, Realtor*
*Windward Real Estate Agency*

And there you have it. Does everyone respond to this? Oh, heavens no! But the response is high enough that it makes the research worthwhile. By the end of February, I was following up with both phone calls and in-person visits. In March, I began showing available properties and contacting other upscale owners to suggest it was a good time to sell and that I had a potential buyer. My pipeline was filling.

———— ❧ ————

It's good to make money while you can. I had the assistance of my four rookies and Dan had determined not to hire any more until fall. I reviewed every piece of mail they sent, visited every open house they held, and brainstormed every marketing plan with them. And they were doing well. The checks they received at the end of the year had kept them working into spring and they were actually turning some property. They also assisted me with events and marketing my high-end products.

I had a booth at the Home Show, the RV Show, and the Boat Show. These were the major shows that wealthy people seemed to attend. They were upgrading their homes, getting ready to retire and move on, or adding a significant status upgrade. I worked the busiest hours, but the rookies were getting referrals as well.

Unfortunately, the hottest real estate season meant my studio sat empty, even on my 'weekend' days of Monday and Tuesday. I was too tired to paint. Things have a tendency to balance out in the long run, though.

——— ⁂ ———

"MR. PETERS, YOU seem to be the first thing my wife and I have agreed on in two years. There is hope for the future," Mr. Barrett said when we sat to discuss their purchase needs. He'd just been promoted to Vice President in a local high-tech company. Not 'THE' Vice President, he was quick to tell me. Just 'A' vice president.

"It hasn't been quite that bad," Mrs. Barrett said. "But it does keep life interesting."

"I hope I can help you come to an agreement regarding your new home," I said. Contrary to the comment, the couple seemed to get along incredibly well. She was very down-to-earth and I could see she grounded him. And they were well-matched in age. This was no trophy wife. She was the real deal and had been with him through thick and thin. He honored that.

We met for over an hour as I probed for what they really wanted. Sometimes it seems a real estate agent needs to be part psychologist. They also gave me a tour of their home and I took photos so I could work up a good estimate on its market value. I met their two children, both of whom seemed eager to move to a new and bigger house. They gave me some input regarding what they wanted, including a big yard so they could have a dog. The elder Barretts smiled indulgently.

"Oh, there is one other thing," Mrs. Barrett said, nudging her husband. I was at the door and ready to leave. Mr. Barrett seemed a little embarrassed.

"Your name came up in another context during a dinner we had with Keith and Louise Brainerd. You are the artist who painted Louise's portrait, aren't you?" Mr. Barrett asked.

"Yes. That piece was done some ten years ago."

"But you are still painting, aren't you?" Mrs. Barrett asked.

"Certainly. This season makes it a little difficult to find the time as I'm trying to get the best real estate deals for my clients, but I do find

136

some time to paint and do portraits," I said.

"Well, as you look for a new home for us, keep in mind that we'll want a place to display the portrait of Donna that we'd like you to paint," Mr. Barrett said. "That is, if you are still doing commissions."

"I'll definitely keep that in mind," I said. Mrs. Barrett gave me a shy smile.

⸻ ⚬ ⸻

Easter Sunday afternoon, Rita came into my studio as I was flipping through sketches, looking for more material. She brought one of my portfolios over and sat on my lap as we opened it and perused the sketches. It was an older portfolio and I hadn't seen these pictures in a good ten years or more. Rita tried to guess which models I'd slept with based on my drawings, but I told her that wasn't likely, simply because I seldom slept with a model before I had done the sketches, and usually not until after a painting was finished. Still, she was uncannily correct in most of her assessments.

It's not that I sleep with all my models, or even a majority of them. I don't. There has to be a special spark that connects us. It wasn't until I painted *Pain is Pleasure* in my newer style that I'd been moved by a sexual experience before I painted. I'd never seen Kelly when I painted *Out of Body*, though we'd had sex. *Cold Fusion* was painted months after my experience with Sheila and I had pleasured her but didn't go all the way. It wasn't until the two most recent paintings of Lori that I'd approached the canvas with every intention of sleeping with the model. That was at Rita's instigation.

And Rita was looking for signs of raw passion that I could interpret anew in a painting. I was certainly not going back ten years or more to track down a model with the intent of having sex so I could paint her. Our relationship had long since left the "teaching" of the art of love behind. She approached looking at the sketches with an eye toward formulating an experiment. We were laughing and I had reached the point of wanting to try another posed portrait with her when I heard her breath catch.

When I realized what sketch she was looking at, I held my breath, awaiting the explosion.

"Oh. My. God." Rita got up from my lap, carrying the sketch with her. I squeezed my eyes shut and tried to think how I would explain this. The portfolio was over ten years old, right? That particular sketch was one of the earliest pieces I did in my studio, maybe fourteen years ago. Rita was what? Twelve?

"You slept with her, didn't you?" she asked without looking back at me. I chose not to confirm or deny, but stayed silent. She carried the sketch to my modeling stage and began arranging furniture on it. She quickly found the wicker chair that was in the picture, though I'd refinished it and it was no longer white. She went to the blanket box where I kept various drapes and brought out a knitted afghan. She looked at the pattern, comparing it to the sketch before bringing it to her nose to inhale deeply.

That was a waste of effort. Once a drape has been used, I always had it laundered or cleaned. I couldn't remember having used that particular one since the sketch she held. It had been at the bottom of the box a long time.

She arranged the chair and afghan along with a wooden stool and a bowl for fruit on the platform. I left the studio while she worked, knowing what she would want next. I returned with a selection of apples, oranges, a pear, and bananas. She took them from me and smiled. The smile did nothing to set me at ease. If anything, it was predatory. She arranged the fruit in the bowl like it had been in the sketch, then stepped back off the platform to look at the setting from the perspective of the sketch. Since her initial question, neither of us had spoken a word. She went to my supply cabinet and found a sketchbook the same size and texture as the paper in her hands, and gave it to me. I understood what was about to happen—or what I thought was about to happen—I glanced at the sketch again and went to get a selection of graphite, erasers, and a tortillon. When I returned to my position and faced the platform, Rita was nude, sitting in the chair with the throw across her lap and one foot on the stool. Her hand was poised over the fruit bowl, head lowered seductively and facing me. I knew my role. I sketched.

"All these years, I never knew," she said as I worked. Her shape was incredible, and seeing her in that position brought a flood of memories. I was so young and full of myself. I thought my first paintings would sell for a fortune and I'd paint only for pleasure. That sketch was only for pleasure, completed after we'd been lovers for several weeks. But even when I did it, I knew we wouldn't last.

"Did you love her as much as it looks in the sketch?"

"Yes." The shadows dipped beneath her breast and blended into the dark edge of the afghan. With a few flicks of the tortillon, the pattern emerged from the knitting. The fruit was round and lush. The detail in the wicker was sharp—perhaps sharper than what I actually saw.

"Why? Why did you break up?"

"The age difference. The stages of our lives. The fears and inabilities. Our own doubts. The inequality of what we each brought to the relationship. My inexperience." They were all reasons. No one thing had come between us, but everything had conspired against us. I looked at the sketch in my hands, not knowing if I could go on. The patterns, fruit, props—all were complete. But the figure—Rita—was still missing.

"Were you thinking of her when you made love to me?" It was only a whisper but I heard and could not answer. Rita's voice rose slightly to be sure I could hear her, but was still below her normal conversational tone. "Did you think of her breasts when you caressed my skin? Did you smell her scent when you went down on me? Did you feel her lips when I sucked you? Hear her sighs when I came?"

It was too much. I dropped the sketchbook with its incomplete figure on the floor and my pencils scattered around me. I stood, ready to flee, but Rita stood before me, pressing her lips to mine, pulling my arms around her. When I pulled back to look into her eyes, the pain I felt was mirrored there.

"No," I said simply. "Until this night, I never thought of her when I was with you. Until you found that sketch, I thought I had left her behind."

"Then now—tonight—you can remember her the way she was." Rita picked up my sketch and laid it gently on the stool. "Make love to me, here in the studio. Let me be her in your arms tonight. Then finish the sketch. Do the painting. Put her in it, the way you remember her. Let her come to life in your hands. Do it for me, Doc. Do it for us."

We moved to the daybed. Rita dragged the afghan to cushion us and we made love. It was nothing fancy. We simply kissed with her draped partially on top of me until she shifted over me and we slid together. She rode on top, fully pressed against me as we kissed. I felt her climax, the muscles in her pussy tightening around my cock, even as she kept up her steady rhythm. I felt the sudden gasp as the sensations became too much for her and I marveled again at the intensity she brought to our lovemaking. Then, for a few moments, she lifted her head from mine and simply looked into my eyes, coaxing me to come inside her.

And come, I did. I never moved a muscle but let her milk me with her pussy, drawing out everything I could give her. I held her to me as tightly as I could and saw my tears in her eyes as we both wept. Sometime—minutes or hours later—Rita rose, letting me slide out of her silky chamber. She kissed me softly once again as she gathered up her clothing.

"Paint her, Doc. Paint my mom the way we remember her."

— 🙚 —

WHEN I MOVED into this house, I held a party and invited all my neighbors to meet the young kid who'd just joined the community. The first guests to arrive were Rose and her two daughters, Rita and Tina. The girls were nine and eleven years old. Rose was a single mom about ten years older than me. She had the struggles all young single parents have but they were somewhat alleviated by living with her mother next door. We were good neighbors but within six months we were more than that. We were so afraid that someone would find out we were meeting and were sexually involved that she would leave the girls with her mom and drive to the local shopping center. I'd pick her up there and we'd drive to my house, pulling into the garage and closing the door before she got out. Then we would drink wine and laugh for hours, sometimes making love in front of the fireplace, in the bed, in the studio—sometimes just cuddling on the sofa until it was time to take her back to her car so she could arrive home without anyone knowing she'd been next door.

I suspected her mom, Miriam, knew. But in the three months we were together, we never appeared in public with each other. The strain got to be too much. She couldn't face going public with a relationship with a man ten years younger. I was only fifteen years older than her daughters.

I'd sketched her in the studio, but our lovemaking always interfered with my ability to paint her, so a canvas was never completed.

Nearly five years later, she was diagnosed with breast cancer. Despite her treatments, having her beautiful breasts removed, going bald with chemotherapy and radiation, she succumbed in just four months. The entire neighborhood was in shock. The girls, then fourteen and sixteen, were devastated. I grieved in silence for what we almost had. That was twelve years ago now. I never thought of Rose in my time with Rita. Now I could think of nothing else.

⸻ ❧ ⸻

THERE WERE COLORS I'd never used in my palette before that splashed across the painting of Rose. The afghan, dulled by age, was suddenly bright and vibrant. Her skin glowed with health and energy. Her breasts were round and full and her expression one of contemplated mischief. And through the entire time I painted on Monday and Tuesday, there were tears in my eyes. I didn't see the painting clearly until Friday when Rita joined me.

We stood together in front of the painting and held each other as if we were at a wedding altar. There were tears, but it was a joyful occasion. Standing with Rita felt like we were receiving a blessing from the long-dead mother in the painting.

"It's somehow comforting to think that she knows how I feel and is happy for us," Rita said. "Can we spend the weekend in bed?"

"Until Monday morning. I have a portrait sitting."

"Who?"

"Donna Barrett. I'm trying to find a new home for her and her husband. Two children under twelve. Strange couple. They saw the article in *Home Spectacular* and happen to be friends with the Brainerds. They decided they want a painting of Mrs. Barrett to hang in their new home when they have it."

"Sex on the outlook?" Rita asked brightly.

"Oh, no. Not with this one," I said. "They have a strange relationship. He said choosing me to find their new home was the first thing they'd agreed on in two years. But there was no sign at all of their relationship deteriorating. They were quite loving."

"Always keep an open mind," Rita giggled. "Now let's eat. I brought Thai food. Then you can take me to bed and see how long you can keep me there."

⚷

It was a great weekend. Not that we spent all our time fucking, but we did spend the majority of it in bed. We read, talked, played games, made love. And by the end of the weekend, Rita had agreed to fully move in. She'd been spending four or five nights a week with me but was still nominally living next door. This week, she planned a full move.

Monday morning, I was ready in my studio for Donna Barrett. I greeted her at ten and served tea and cookies while we talked about what kind of portrait she wanted. She was distracted by my paintings and wandered around the studio looking at them. I'd hung all eight of them in the studio, which took about all my wall space since some of them were so large. I'd hung *Adoration* and *Blessing* next to each other—Tina with little baby Rachel, and Rose. Donna was fixated on them.

"These paintings are completely different than Louise's portrait," Donna said. "I'd almost think they were done by a different artist."

"I discovered this style and technique just a year ago. I still paint portraits, however."

"Can you paint my portrait in this style? Louise would be so jealous," Donna laughed. "Not that I want her to be jealous, but this is so much more vibrant. I can't picture myself in a plain portrait now."

"Um… Well… these painting come from an intense emotional connection. The one I tried to paint that was missing that just didn't have the life these do."

"Oh. And I see they are all nudes. Did you make love to all of them?" she asked. If this was what Mr. Barrett faced at dinner every night, no wonder he said they hadn't agreed on anything in two years. Still, not only was she a portrait client, I thought I might have a lead on the perfect house for them. I didn't want to screw this up.

"Not all of them." Certainly not Tina and baby Rachel. And I'd done the steam room painting from imagination.

"Hmm. Would you mind if I asked my husband to stop by while we talk and perhaps begin sketching? I've an idea and I think he will want input."

"Of course. Why don't we start with a few simple sketches in a standard portrait mode? You can tell me about your idea while I get used to your features in a sketch," I said. Whatever the idea, I was sure it didn't involve sex and couldn't imagine it involving nudity, so I wasn't concerned about her husband visiting.

———————

CLIVE BARRETT SHOWED up in time for lunch and was kind enough to bring sushi from Ryuko Sushi Bar. I'd made a quick call to Rita and she agreed to come home for lunch as well. I brewed a pot of green tea to have with the delicacies and we sat at the dining room table. When Clive had arrived, I took care of setting the table and Donna took her husband to the studio to show him my paintings and the sketches we'd accomplished that morning.

"I can certainly see why Donna wants her portrait done in this new style of yours," Clive said. "The difference between this and the older portraits we saw is amazing. We'd like to discover what kind of connection it takes to get that far. We're not swingers, but we are a bit more liberal in our practices than you might think."

"Please understand that Doc doesn't do these paintings in order to have sex with the model," Rita said. I'd introduced her as my lovely assistant and she took on the role of my business manager. "When we first discovered this breakthrough, I began arranging experiments to see what triggered the connection you are referring to. Initially, I thought it was just the sexual experience, but further study showed that was not the only trigger. For example, the painting *Adoration* of the mother and baby was inspired simply from being with my family at Thanksgiving. That's my sister and her baby. The portrait next to it, painted just last week, is of my mother. She's been gone for ten years now. I posed for it."

"So, there is a possibility of developing the connection without explicitly having sex," Donna probed. "What have you discovered is the key?"

"I think the best illustration is *Out of the Fog*," Rita continued. "It is based on a story I told Doc. Of course, I set the stage if you will, by taking him to the shower and steaming things up as I told him about an encounter I had at the gym. But we never actually touched during the telling of the story. He painted the image from memory and imagination."

"A story? Donna, that rings a bell," Clive said.

"Indeed. You see, Doc, I'm not only a stay-at-home mom. I'm a writer. I think I might have a story that would inspire you," Donna said.

"And let me say that we agreed to a price of $5,000 for the portrait. If you can interpret Donna in the style you are showing in your studio, I'll double that amount."

"There would be one other consideration," Rita said. I don't think I'd said anything since we sat down to eat. "Doc is preparing for an exhibition within the next year. Any paintings done in this style must be made available for the show. Not for sale, of course. Just to help fill out the exhibition. Can we agree to that?"

"I don't see a problem," Clive said. "Donna will work with you as often as necessary. She may pose with or without clothes. If anything develops beyond that, I will not know. You need have no crises of conscience. Is that agreeable?"

"Understanding that we don't yet know if I can create the connection and paint in this style, I'm in agreement," I said at last. This was going to make it very hard to work in real estate for the next month.

# 16
# Dark Shadows

I MET MONDAYS AND Tuesdays with Donna for the next two weeks. I'd filled half a dozen sketchbooks as we talked. She told me stories of her family and childhood, her relationship with Clive—which had been ongoing since they were sophomores in high school—her children, and finally, her writing. I didn't need to do much prompting in our conversations as Donna was a natural storyteller. I was surprised it took so long to get around to what was obviously her passion. Her whole demeanor changed when she started talking about writing.

"Clive told me when we were still just kids that he'd earn a living and support me so I could write. And he has," she said. "Of course, writing isn't the only thing I do. I make damn sure Clive thinks the deal was a bargain for him. If he wants a blowjob and I haven't already offered, I'm on my knees before he finishes the thought. My house is always spotless and I make sure he has dinner when he gets home. If he's late, I keep it warm. If he's early, I fix a cocktail. If he's horny, I fuck him."

"It sounds like a good deal for him," I said. "Has it been worth it to you?" I looked up at her again to reference my sketch and saw her blouse was gapping open a bit. I nearly said something when I realized she was unfastening another button. I kept my peace.

"It's a great deal for me. Not only do I get plenty of time to write, I have a great sex life! And Clive knows he's got a good deal. He does everything possible to keep me happy at home. And he is a constant part of the kids' lives. You might think this is strange, but Clive doesn't really have any hobbies. He doesn't go out drinking with the boys. He doesn't spend weekends playing golf. He isn't part of a Lions Club or Kiwanis. The kids and I are his hobby. He spends his free time with us." Her blouse was fully unbuttoned now and I could see one bra covered breast.

"What was the deal telling me I was the first thing you'd agreed on in two years?" I asked.

"Oh, a happy couple needs some kind of conflict to overcome. I play a silly game online at one of my publishers. It's called 'This or That' which puts up two things to choose between. It could be 'Hotdogs or hamburgers?' 'Vacation at the beach or vacation in the mountains?' 'Cat or dog?' It's just a silly preference thing, but we play the game together. We had a near perfect record of disagreeing until we narrowed down our choice of Realtor to you or Candace Higgins. We both chose you."

"I'm flattered. I hope it doesn't spell an end to your disagreements," I laughed. Donna's blouse was off and her bra was unfastened, hanging loosely over her breasts. I loved the slope into her cleavage and quickly did a sketch of just her breasts. I'd want to examine this more closely.

"Oh, we haven't agreed on anything since we chose you. Well, except the portrait. It would be hard to disagree about that." She reached to her right for the bottle of water on the end table and her bra slid off her arms and onto the floor. I kept drawing.

Donna wasn't the most beautiful woman I'd ever seen. I mean, Rita. But she was good looking in the way of a woman who takes care of herself but doesn't obsess over weight, hairstyle, or manicure. I shifted my stool so I could get a better angle for my sketch. Donna tried a couple of poses that I pulled together. Her breasts were soft and hung slightly, though they weren't so big as to be weighed down by gravity. The nipples and areolae were dark, in contrast to her fair complexion. She'd become distracted by something on the other side of the room and I sketched her while she was focused over there. The intense look on her face was a stark contrast to the casual exposure of her breasts.

My alarm beeped and I looked up at the big clock. Three o'clock.

"I lost track of time," she said. "This was such an interesting session. Sadly, I need to break it off now to be home for the kids." She stood up and zipped up the side of her skirt. I hadn't even noticed it was unfastened and obviously next scheduled for departure. She absently tugged her bra on, looking over my shoulder as I flipped through the day's sketches. She was quite casual about dressing and in no hurry to cover herself. She pointed at one of the later sketches. I agreed, there was something about that one with her attention focused on the other side of the room. "I think we're getting closer to that connection," she whispered.

She finished pulling herself together, said goodbye, and left. I looked at the sketch again. *Yes, closer.*

⁂

On Saturday, the family followed me to a house in Sun Eden Estates. This wasn't a gated community like Holly Park, but the properties were, indeed, estates. Each was on a minimum of two acres and had plenty of parking for guests. The houses were large and designed to entertain. The house we were viewing was slightly over 5,000 square feet.

It wasn't for sale. Yet.

Some diligent footwork and follow-up with past clients had led me to the Jerry Dickinson family. Jerry had recently been laid off in a massive change of regime at a Fortune 100 manufacturing company. He'd been Executive Vice President but when the Board cleaned house in the wake of a drop in sales, Jerry was one of the dozen top level casualties. My source indicated that he'd been recruited by a company on the Coast and would probably want to move soon.

When I contacted him, I found that he'd already taken the job in San Jose and was commuting on a weekly basis. He'd already missed two of his regularly scheduled weekends home and wanted his family to join him as quickly as possible. His three children were opposed to the move, not wanting to leave friends and classmates. But he'd promised they could finish out the year at their present schools. I was invited to do a market evaluation of the home and it helped that I already had a prospective buyer.

Clive and Donna entered through the massive entry arch over the front door and stopped just inside. To the left of the foyer was a sunken living room with a cozy fireplace and high ceilings. To the right was a curved staircase descending from an overhead balcony that bridged a passage to the gallery. Here, one could move into the kitchen and dining room or the study/library on the other side. Directly ahead was a massive stone fireplace that opened on both the gallery side and the great room beyond. It was a lot to take in and I let them simply stare for a few minutes without trying to point anything out to them.

They became more and more enthused as they toured the house. The great room was a big hit as a potential entertainment space that opened to the library -office on one side and the dining room on the other. They were quite enthused about the partially hidden staircase from the library up to the master bedroom suite. Across the bridge over the foyer, were three more bedrooms with en suite baths. The kids loved the layout. A large open space was equipped with games and a large screen TV.

They had several whispered conversations and paused for a long time in the impressive foyer before turning to me again.

"There," Donna pointed toward the gallery and the massive stone fireplace. "That is where my portrait will hang." In their minds, they'd already bought the house. "And here is where I'll pose," she continued, pointing to the staircase. I smiled. I could see her in a long dressing gown as she descended the stairs like a movie star. She broke the illusion by giggling.

"Is there a 'that' we can compare it to?" Clive asked.

"At the moment, I've found 'this.' The comparison is the home you are currently in."

"This," they both said.

Of course, there was some negotiating to do. The $2.7 million price was a shock, but I'd already done a market evaluation of their current home at $1.5 million. When you reach that level, moving up $1.2 million isn't that big a step. I represented both sides of the deal and went over the market proposal and comparable properties with both couples. They agreed on a price of $2.5 million. The Dickinsons wanted to stay for two more months while their kids finished school—an easy concession for the Barretts. I could list their house immediately and start looking for a buyer. Since I did not need to do any further marketing of the Dickinson house, I reduced my commission to six percent, which I would still need to split with my broker, Dan. Dan and I wouldn't make an easier $75,000 each any time soon.

The Dickinson family was spending the long Memorial Day weekend in San Jose as they finalized a purchase there. I'm afraid they wouldn't get anywhere near as impressive a house in California for the price. But they agreed that I could work that weekend with Donna, preparing the pose and sketching her portrait in the foyer.

⎯⎯⎯3†8⎯⎯⎯

RITA BOUNCED INTO my studio the first of May. There is no other word for the way she arrived. She brought energy and enthusiasm everyplace she went. Living with her was the highlight of my life. We often spent our evenings nude, and I'd completed a sketch on paper of the first pose I'd done of her when she came to my house for 'lessons' in the art of love. She'd twice brought home 'experiments' for me to sketch after a bout of serious lovemaking. They weren't universally successful, but she documented the results as if she were doing a doctoral dissertation on my art and style.

On this day, Rita was particularly happy.

"Guess what," she started, but didn't let me reply. "I have a gallery interested in your showing." That was a shock. I still had only nine pieces in my new and improved style. I would need at least a dozen for a good gallery show. Of course, there were more mundane pieces I could show and sketches that could be prepared for display, but I wasn't sure I wanted to mix my previous style with the new works.

"I'm not ready for a showing."

"I know. I didn't say she wanted the show this month. She's thinking about a fall or winter show. I showed her the digitals of your work and she wants to see them up close. We're supposed to meet her on Monday."

"Not this Monday," I said. I was still in shock that a gallery was interested. "I have a portrait sitting Monday."

"Really? I thought you weren't doing Donna until Memorial Day weekend. Who?"

"Ardith Longfellow."

"Do I know her?"

"Only from the society pages. She's quite the philanthropist and is often at the fundraisers for the orchestra, theater, and ballet. The art museum, in fact, has commissioned a painting of her for their Benefactors Gallery. It will be a good way to get my name out in a museum."

"Yes, but in the wrong way!"

"I'll make it work somehow," I said. I had no idea how that was going to play out. I'd met the woman only once when I toured the museum. Ardith Longfellow had a mind of her own and a will of iron. But Rita agreed to get the owner of the gallery to wait until the weekend. I could possibly try Ardith's portrait in the new style. It would be good practice for painting Donna.

———❧———

"I WANT EVERY wrinkle, scar, and mole in this painting," Ardith said to me in a somewhat querulous voice. The woman was over seventy years old and had ruled the arts scene for nearly fifty of them. I simply couldn't believe what she was asking.

She stood before me without a stitch of clothing. I'd told her to make herself comfortable in the studio as I went to get tea. When I returned, she was standing with a helmet on her head, greaves on her legs, and a sword in her hand. She wore nothing else.

Over the course of the next five hours, I did many sketches as she posed. I finally managed to get her to add the traditional shield to her outfit, allowing her breasts and crotch to be partially, though not fully covered. I explained it was often better to leave a bit to the imagination. She laughed at me. During the time we worked, she told me story after story about her life and how she had earned her wrinkles. She told me of her loves, her children, her projects.

I wasn't sure the art museum would accept a full-length nude of her for the Benefactors Gallery. I'd toured it to prepare for this painting and the portraits were standard head and shoulders, some down to mid-torso. I suggested that we do two portraits, one with the full regalia and one more traditional.

"I'm sick and tired of everything considered beautiful and womanly having to be twenty years old. I want a proud portrait of this aging body put on display where everyone can see it. Like that one." She pointed to the painting of Rose. "Just not so bright and lively. I want a brooding darkness in my visage. And my eyes. When people look into my eyes, they should see every man and woman I slept with to rise to the top of the arts world. Money alone will not suffice to become influential. I've fought and scrapped for every advancement in the arts community I've brought about. I offered five million dollars for a new children's wing in the art museum, only to find out half of it would go in the pockets of the executive director and architect. I commissioned my own architects, bought property, and had a new children's museum built from the ground up. It cost three times what I'd offered for the new wing, but not a penny went into the greedy hands of those who live off the blood of true artists."

"Perhaps I could paint you with the Gorgon's head clasped in one hand," I joked.

"Do you think you could make it so it would turn viewers to stone?" she asked. I thought for a minute she was serious. "I've heard you are the best local portrait artist. I wasn't certain when I saw your portfolio. Your portraits are all fine, high quality paintings. But none of them have the snap and verve of what I see on your studio walls. What happened?"

"I discovered a different level of my art when I made an emotional connection with my model," I said simply. "It is difficult to produce on demand, but I'm discovering new ways to make the connection. I believe I can paint you in that style if it is what you want." Ardith laid down her sword and shield and took off the helmet. She looked over my shoulder at the most recent sketch and I moved aside to let her flip through the pages.

"You are learning to make the connection even without benefit of sex. I would definitely fuck you if it was necessary to get this level of artistry. I'm afraid, however, that the connection you made would be one of disgust and pain." She pulled my hand to her floppy breast. "I've given suck to three children and countless little boys disguised as powerful men." She dragged my hand down and placed it between her legs. "I hold a sword, but my weapon of choice has always been my sheath. I can be pierced there and still be victorious." She brought my hand to her face. "But here—these dry lips and wrinkled lines—here is where power must show through."

We turned back to the sketches and she finally chose two. One was an early sketch from our session with her standing armed and ready for battle. In the other, she knelt with the helmet on the ground in front of her, shield covering much of her body, sword pointed at the ground. It was a pose of rest, not defeat nor surrender. It was an image of the woman preparing herself for the next battle.

"This one for the gallery," she said. "The other, paint freely and with joy. For me. I will find the right place to display it. Do good work, Doc. I'm tired now and need to go home."

Frankly, there is little harder to paint than perfectly smooth, flawless skin. As marvelous as it is to look at and delightful to caress, on canvas it inevitably looks flat and lifeless. But give me a figure with a little character—some lines around her eyes, a sagging breast, gray in her pussy hair, and a bit of a wattle—and we are in heaven. What's more, as I sketched and she talked, I began to see her in a new light. I saw her as the accomplished matron warrior she wanted to play. She had, indeed, faced life's battles and won.

—— ﷼ ——

"DID YOU FUCK her?"

"No." Though I had been thinking to myself as I was completing the final sketch that I wouldn't turn this woman down if she suggested anything.

"These sketches are amazing. I love this one!" The sketch in question showed Ardith Longfellow kneeling with helmet and shield in front of her and sword held point down. Her hair was a frazzled mass of gray curls, somewhat matted by the time beneath her helm. As I'd positioned the shield, Dear Ms. Longfellow had made sure her sagging breast made contact with the back of my hand. I was amazed to feel the softness of her skin.

"In June," Rita said, putting the sketches aside. At first, I thought she meant I should fuck Ardith in June but Rita finally continued. "The gallery. We have something special in mind for you."

"I thought the owner wanted to see my paintings."

"There's time for that after we've met. I thought you should see the gallery first… in a manner of speaking."

"In a manner of speaking?"

"Yes." Rita grinned at me. "It's a little experiment she agreed to let me conduct. It will give you the full experience of her gallery to see if you think it's a fit."

Rita's little experiments tended to be too sexual for most gallery owners to participate in, so I was a little skeptical. She continued to press, stating it was an experiment with sculptures. She gave me a catalog of the current exhibition, called "Modern Renaissance," and I could see the bronze and marble statues were closely patterned after the classic works of the sixteenth century. I finally agreed to a date in June, not knowing how seeing a bunch of sculpture would help me with either my painting or the proposed exhibition.

In the meantime, I had paintings to finish.

# 17
## Stony Silence

SATURDAY MORNING OF Memorial Day weekend, I met Donna at what would be her new home. During the course of the prior month, she'd become good friends with Mrs. Dickinson, who had become an enthusiastic co-conspirator for the portrait. I had a signed permission slip to work in the house over the weekend.

I moved my easel and charcoals into the space and got myself situated while Donna prepared her scene and costume.

"Are you ready?" she asked from the top of the stairs.

"Whenever you are, Donna."

"Okay. Well. Then here I come."

What crept silently down the stairs was an image from a 1940s horror film. Or perhaps a pulp novel cover.

She wore a filmy peignoir with nothing under it. She had high-heeled slippers and a gun clutched in her hand. The peignoir appeared to have been pulled on in haste, belted, but not completely closed. One shoulder was bare where it slipped down. She stopped a few steps from the bottom and looked out past my left where the gun vaguely pointed.

"Wow!" I said. "Just stay exactly like that for a moment." I hastily drew a charcoal sketch on my first page. Before I'd sketched Ardith, I'd put in an entire ream (500 sheets) of Strathmore 300 Charcoal Paper. It was a nice heavy 64-pound paper and was cut in 25x38-inch sheets. The laid finish took charcoal and soft graphite extremely well. And I'd discovered I really needed the larger sketch paper when I was working on paintings the size I'd recently been doing. Ardith's museum portrait would be thirty inches wide and four feet high. Her warrior painting would be twice that height. I'd carefully measured the display space in the Barretts' new home and had determined I could fit a framed portrait as much as three feet wide and four feet tall over the fireplace.

In the time it has taken me to describe the technical aspects of my drawing paper, I'd already completed two sketches of Donna. I moved my easel between sketches to capture her from a different angle. I liked what I saw. Which was pretty much everything.

"I write romantic thrillers," she said as I completed the second sketch. "I might want to use this painting as a book cover for my new work, *On My Own*."

"May I try positioning you a little differently?"

"Certainly."

The position of her feet, both on one step, baffled the tension. When I had her shift her left foot down a step, the tension in her pose increased palpably. So did the exposure of her private parts, which had no other covering. I wondered if she'd chosen the trimmed style that left just a triangle of pubic hair pointing directly at her slit. In the process of shifting her weight, the robe had slipped down farther off her right shoulder and exposed her breast.

"I'd like to get a sketch in this pose. Raise your chin slightly. Tell me, are you terrified of what you might find when you come down the stairs or confident that you can handle it?"

"Confident. I probably won't want to be so completely exposed on the book cover, but show me what it's like."

"Believe me, it's stunning. Now, gun raised to the right in your left hand. Right hand on the banister. You're not left-handed, are you?"

"I can shoot with either hand."

That gave me pause. She certainly held the gun comfortably and having moved up close to position her, I could tell it was no stage prop or toy. I fell to work sketching in far more detail than my first two.

"Tell me about your heroine."

"It's summed up when she confronts him about his knight in shining armor complex," she said. "I'm much stronger than you, Percy. Oh, you can outlift me with brute strength, but you are weak in fortitude. A woman would die a thousand deaths waiting for you to rescue her. I'd much rather depend on myself."

"That's definitely a confident woman," I said.

"The heroines in my novels rescue themselves when they are in trouble. Sometimes they rescue the man as well. We aren't weak women who need a man to come to our aid," Donna said.

"At the same time, you are sexy and passionate, able to love more deeply and defend more valiantly."

"Have you been reading my books?"

"I confess I have not, but I believe I will. You can pull yourself together and let's take a break for a few minutes. There are a couple of other poses I'd like to try that will better capture those characteristics and be a little more subtle in your exposure."

We worked the entire day. I had a selection of poses to choose from and might very well paint a second image—one of the more exposed—for myself. It was getting dark. We'd eaten a light dinner Rita had packed for us and discussed the dynamic of the character in her new book. What I was missing was the dynamic of the dark and somewhat spooky night.

"Can you continue to work for a while?"

"All night if you wish, Doc. I've come up with some additional concepts for stories while we have been talking. I find it… stimulating," she said. That was an interesting choice of words.

"I'd like to try backlighting you a bit and now that it's dark out, I think I can work with a limited light. Let's put a lamp at the head of the stairs. I won't include it in the sketch, but I'll try using it for lighting. I've a couple of clip lights that I'll use to light my sketch pad."

We returned to our positions and I arranged her the way I wanted her on the stairs. Donna had become quite free with how she encouraged me to touch her. I found that positioning her peignoir over her breast might take two or three minutes as I smoothed it out against her nipple.

The result of the new lighting and pose was even sexier than when she was fully exposed. Backlit like she was, her body was silhouetted in the filmy robe. We definitely got the pose and lighting right for her figure, but her face was too dark. I sketched anyway and on a sudden inspiration, turned one of my drawing lights around to face her. It was just enough light on her face that I could capture the detail of her face. Being just slightly below her, the shadows did interesting things as well.

By ten-thirty, I was satisfied. Donna approached my easel and I set all the day's sketches on it. I pushed myself back and she immediately perched herself on my lap to review the sketches. Perhaps it was the easiest place to see them from, but I could have moved.

She made a running commentary about the sketches and how she'd felt as each was being drawn. When we got to the series in which she was fully exposed she pulled my hand up under her peignoir to her breast.

"My heroine is strong enough to control an interaction or to abide by the consequences if she is unable to. The murderer lurking below might see her exposed, but it will make no difference in her confidence. She does not need clothes to face danger. And should he get the drop on her, she will endure his hands on her body, delving into her most intimate depths, biding her time until she can turn the distraction of her body against her foe and subdue him."

During this narration, she'd guided my hand down her torso and between her legs. She let me play there for some time as her arousal increased and she continued to page through the sketches. At last she reached the backlit sketch with her face in low light. She turned her face and kissed me as I worked on her sex with my fingers.

"This. This one. You have captured me the way I wish to be seen." She mounted quickly to a low-pitched keen and her pussy tightened around my fingers. "Go. Go paint me, Doc."

SHE DRESSED. I picked up my supplies. We left the house.

I stayed up the rest of the night working on the prepared canvas. I caught a couple of hours' sleep just before dawn and Rita woke me with coffee and breakfast. She kissed me soundly and said she was spending the day with her sister. I returned to the studio and began applying layers of heavy paint for the background in which the staircase and background were distinguished by strokes of my palette knife rather than color. In the foreground emerged the woman, backlit as if she were, herself, a ghost on the stairs. Her face glowed with confidence— the expression, one of determination. Hints of the shape of her breasts and nipples were carved out of the filmy gauze of her peignoir but the hand on her gun was steady and sure.

IN ADDITION TO the portraits, I had two additional paintings to do: Ardith as the warrior goddess and Donna as the exposed heroine. It took me the next two weeks, while the paint on the portraits cured, for me to finish the paintings. I was ready for a break… I thought.

Rita woke me early Sunday with coffee but immediately wagged her butt toward me as she headed for the shower. I followed. She stayed at her own end of the shower, though, quickly rinsing and drying herself. I followed suit and dressed in the clothes she laid out for me. We got in her Cabriolet, but it was still much too cold to have the top down.

"Will you trust me to handle today? Put yourself in my hands and let me guide you where you should go?" I smiled. The first request made me think she wanted to negotiate terms, but I quickly realized she was staging one of her experiments. They were always interesting, to say the least.

"Your wish is my command," I acquiesced.

"Then let's put this on," she said. She put a sleep mask over my eyes and sealed it with a vinyl head mask that left me completely blind, though this time I could hear and my nose and mouth were clear.

"You'll have the use of your senses of touch, smell, hearing, and taste, but not sight, during this experiment. I'll lead you to each sculpture and you will be able to explore the artist's work through your hands and body."

We drove about twenty minutes to the gallery and she led me into the building. She seated me in a comfortable lobby chair and whispered that she would return as soon as she made sure everything was ready. By my estimate, it was only nine a.m. and most galleries didn't open on Sunday until one. We'd have the gallery undisturbed until then. I wasn't sure how many patrons came to a sculpture exhibit blindfolded, but I was willing to let that thought pass.

While I waited, I let myself observe my environment with my other senses. I could smell a mixture of paint and wood. The paint smells were a few days old. I tried to think what the wood smell reminded me of and suddenly thought of a warehouse. My ears told me the space was large and open, but it didn't tell me much about the surfaces. I shuffled my feet a bit and finally managed to wedge my shoes off and run my sock-covered toes across the floor. It was surprising. It felt like cold, smooth marble. In a few moments, a hand touched my shoulder. I started. I hadn't heard her approach.

"Good. You already have your shoes off," Rita said softly. She wasn't exactly whispering, but she was only using enough volume to be heard, letting me judge again the vastness of the room. She slid my socks off my feet as well. "This will give you another level of sensory input that you don't often use."

Rita led me to sculpture after sculpture, sometimes turning me around in a circle two or three times so I couldn't make a map in my head regarding where each piece was located. I could quickly tell the difference between bronze and stone statues as she named each one. *Western rider. Winged Messenger. Regina.* Then she led me to a sculpture she titled *Veiled Lady.* She always placed my hands where she wanted me to start, then let me explore fully on my own. My hands were placed on soft fabric. I started.

I explored further, expecting to find an actual person beneath my fingers, but soon discovered it was a veil attached to a sculpture. Very funny. On to *Contemplation. Good Governance. Justice. Sapphic Kiss.* On this statue, Rita placed my left hand on a stone breast and my right hand on the neck of a statue. Of course, I moved my hands toward the face, as by the title this seemed to be the place of focus. I traced across the cheek to the lips and felt…

Lips. A pair of very human lips were pressed against the stone of the statue. I let my fingers roam from the stone woman onto the very soft skin of the woman kissing her. Her hair was short. My right hand returned to the head of the stone figure and I discovered she had short hair as well. The living woman did not move a muscle as I traced with one hand down her neck and over her bare shoulder. The other hand mimicked the motion on the sculpture. The bare shoulder gave way to a bare back and on down to a delightfully soft bottom.

As my right hand explored the stone, feeling again the breast where I had started my journey, I crossed the living torso and found a very soft and appealing, warm and sensuous woman's breast pressed against it. I wondered if I would be allowed to continue this exploration and was pleased that as I caressed her breast, there was no movement aside from the expansion of her chest with a deep breath and the sound of a muffled moan from her lips.

Rita then took my hands and pulled me gently away.

"You are not using all your senses," she said softly. She lifted my shirt over my head and I felt her unbuckle my belt. My trousers fell to the floor and she pulled my briefs down with them, pulling them out at the waist to avoid my tumescence. Now naked, I thought I would be returned to the human and stone embrace I had been exploring, but instead, Rita spun me around in circles and led me on to another statue she titled *The Lovers*.

I was keyed now to find flesh beneath my fingers, but instead, my hands were stroking the back of a marble figure. It was male. I don't know how I knew this at once as I hadn't touched either the chest or genitals, but I knew by the feel of the stone, I was touching a man. This was confirmed as I moved my hands around to the front of the statue and encountered his stone partner. She reclined as he bent over her. I ran my hand down to where they were joined. Thinking of Rita's instructions to use all my senses, I joined the embrace of the stone lovers, pressing my body into them and joining my lips to their shared kiss. There was a cold mineral taste as my tongue slipped out to touch where their lips were joined. Rita drew me away again.

"That brings us to *The Three Sisters*," she said. That's a classic theme. Three sisters, sometimes referred to as *The Three Graces*, standing naked in a circle, their arms touching, either dancing or chatting or engaging in some other antic. Sometimes they had water jugs. Sometimes they were pictured with instruments. She led me to a sculpture that was life-size. The cool stone felt incredibly sensuous beneath my fingertips as I stroked the statue's face, shoulders, and torso. The stone breasts were delicate and the artist had detailed nipples beneath a tunic that left one breast exposed. I was amazed at how well I could 'see' the figure through my hands.

I followed the extended right arm of the statue until I encountered a joined hand. This hand, however, like *Sapphic Kiss*, was flesh, not stone. I let my explorations continue, fully expecting to find the same short hair of the woman in that vignette. I was surprised to find long, straight, silky hair. I immediately thought 'Asian' as I felt the bangs of a traditional cut. I stroked down the delicate strands of the hair on her unmoving form and as I reached the end, the back of my hand stroked over an exposed breast. Small, delicate, but with a nipple almost as hard as the stone sculpture to her left. I let my other hand gently stroke her side and discovered the same short tunic, pulled up over one shoulder and a breast. The side was open and I slid my hand behind her, across the bare skin of her back. Still she did not move.

I raised my left hand to her face again, gently tracing the contour of her lips with my thumb. Then I pressed my lips against hers. I could taste the soft mint flavor of her mouth. It was relaxed and her lips were parted slightly, but as I ran my tongue between them, she did not part them further or respond with her own. I continued my exploration with my fingers and my lips, down her extended arm and, despite her immobility, I heard a tiny whimper from her mouth.

The next 'statue' in the trio I recognized by both touch and smell. My lovely assistant Rita was obviously dressed in the same garb, one breast exposed and one barely concealed beneath the flimsy fabric. She held still, but when I bent to suck her tiny exposed nipple into my mouth, she let out a gasp and I felt her hand move to hold my head in place. She guided me to her right with her hand on my head and I left trailing kisses as I moved back toward where the stone figure should be. With two fleshly sisters, I had no real desire to return to the third made of stone. But I found no statue at the end of her fingers.

Instead, my hand grasped open air while my prick was engulfed in a warm wet mouth. Lowering my hand to my waist, I felt the short-cropped hair of the woman who had partnered with Sappho. Now, she was stroking my shaft with hand and mouth while I stood weak-kneed in front of her. My hands were gently removed from her head from behind me and I felt two naked breasts pressed against my back as I was turned.

This time, my hands were moved like a puppet to reach around to the firm small breasts I found in front of me as a delightful round ass backed up against my turgid cock. Still moist from the sucking I'd received, my prick glided up and down between the cheeks as I felt hands stroking my own body and tweaking my nipples. This time there was no static positioning, but active reception of my probing tongue. I was sucked into the mouth that, by the taste, had recently been removed from my cock.

A hand was dragged away from the breast it was stroking and to my left, I found it nestled in a soft wet pussy. I began to smell the scent of arousal all around me as I stroked through the folds. The goddess in front of me turned in my arms and slid down my torso, kissing her way down to my cock, where she inhaled it.

At the same time, I was pushed back to lie in a stony embrace of a statue while another hard but fleshly nipple was pressed between my lips. Moans came from both above my head and from my left where I continued to tickle a clit between my fingers. From the third sister, I heard only the slurping of my cock in her mouth.

And so, it progressed. There were more hands than I thought possible from three women as they continued to turn me around, moving me into scenes with various sculptures, only to discover delightful breasts and pussies, kisses from their lips and caresses of their skin. At one point, I found myself lain across a marble goddess with my cock slick against the cold stone and then I was turned and it was pressed between hot wet pussy lips.

I was settled onto some kind of stone bench, leaning back against the ungiving breasts of a stone woman, while a woman of flesh and blood mounted me and cried out her ecstasy in my ear before sliding away from me again. I was laid back on the bench and mounted at both mouth and cock by two of the goddesses while I felt my toes receive a tongue bath. The sounds and smells of sex, the taste of a pussy in my mouth, the remote mint of a tongue thrust between my lips, the feel of taut, supple skin contrasting with stone beneath my fingers.

And the constant movement. I had no idea how many mouths nor how many pussies my lips and cock had parted. I had no idea where I was when encouraged to embrace bronze or marble statuary. Stone gave way to skin. Bronze slipped into silk. Without my eyes, I was being overwhelmed with sensory input.

I came. I was licked and kissed and caressed back to hardness and I came again. I lost track of my own orgasms and had no hope of counting those of my partners. In my head, stone, bronze, flesh, and fantasy all blended into imagery I couldn't begin to comprehend. My mouth was kissed by lips and tongue and then passed to another and another. Sometimes there were two sets of lips pressed against mine. At one time, I was sure at least three tongues slid across mine and each other's.

So overloaded were my senses, I eventually passed out. I'm sure I was conscious, but I was too overwhelmed to be aware.

———3⁁8———

I awoke to a voice whispering in my ear.

I was in my own bed with no idea how I got there. My entire body still tingled. I was afraid to open my eyes for fear the sensations would dissipate. I was still (again?) naked. I felt a soft hand on my cheek and knew Rita was with me. Her whispered voice came as if from far away as she withdrew.

"Paint."

And then she was gone.

# 18
# Showing

THERE WAS QUITE a crowd. When you have a few influential clients and they let their friends know, and their friends catch a scent of expensive champagne… people just sort of show up. There were only half a dozen galleries in the city big enough to host this showing. When I first walked into this one on the day of our installation, I could smell the scent of fresh paint and old wood. I kicked off my shoes, just so I could walk around on the marble floors of the renovated warehouse in my bare feet. Every step held a memory. In the center of the room, a marble statue of *The Three Sisters* still remained on exhibit, a welcome relief to the walls of paintings.

I was opening with twenty paintings, if you count the fact that three portraits, which were not for sale, were included in the exhibition. All three, however, had corresponding paintings hung that *were* for sale. My painting of *The Three Sisters*, done after Rita's experiment when I was blindfolded in this gallery, was a triptych, three panels, but I counted them as a single painting. The pieces were listed as a unit, but it was completely possible they would be split up sometime in the future. As I wandered through the exhibit before people started arriving, I was surprised to find two of the paintings already marked with 'Sold' signs.

<hr>

I KNEW OF one. The first of the paintings sold had been *Pain is Pleasure.* When Allison got word that I had painted her, she came pounding on my door demanding to see what I'd done.

166

When she saw *Pain is Pleasure*, she stood transfixed for nearly ten minutes. She didn't move a muscle. I finally moved to stand beside her and could see tears streaming down her face. She still didn't move. She didn't make a sound. The tears flowed as though they would never stop. I reached out to dry her cheeks and finally she turned to me.

"You must hate me for what I did to you that night."

"If it weren't for that night, I would never have found the freedom to paint what I have," I answered. "I suppose that if pain is pleasure, then hate might also be love." She melted into my arms and raised her face to me. Her kiss was intense and passionate, but tender. She poured her heart into it as I had poured my soul into the painting.

"You never came back to teach me what making love was like," she said.

"We can remedy that," Rita said from behind us. She set a tray of tea and cookies on the small café table and led us to it. Allison blushed crimson. "Really," Rita continued. "There might even be another painting in it."

Before the week was over, either Rita or I, or both of us, had made love with Allison in every room of her house. We stood beside her as she laid logs in her outdoor fire pit and lit them. When the flames were high, we helped her place her come-stained throw rug on the fire to be consumed.

The painting was already committed to the show, but Allison wrote the gallery a check for $30,000 on the spot. After the show, it would hang above her fireplace.

<hr>

It wasn't long after that I got a call from the gallery to tell me a second painting had been sold based solely on the promotional brochures. Harold Monroe, Sheila's husband, had paid $30,000 for *Cold Fusion*. I called him to thank him for the purchase.

"It's a surprise gift for Sheila's thirty-fifth birthday," he explained. "Not that she doesn't know. She and Allison have been thick as thieves and she told me exactly what she wanted."

"Thank you for agreeing to leave the painting for the show. It was one of the pieces that started me on this style of painting," I said.

"Well, it happens that your show opening coincides with her birthday. Don't be too surprised if the ice queen melts that night. Just enjoy her."

What a strange comment. I wondered if Harold knew all about Sheila's dalliances and perhaps even encouraged them. I'd met people at every end of the social scale during this period of painting. I was sure I would meet more.

⸓

"You should be very proud," Mai Lin Tang said when she called me from the gallery. "We are still two weeks from the show and we are already getting offers based on the brochure. In order to protect your interests, I have changed our pricing schedule. The prices are now listed as 'Reserve Bid' instead of a firm price. Framing has now been completed on the smaller pieces. We won't frame the huge pieces as that could cost as much as the painting itself. Hecate Rising has a reserve bid of $30,000, actually bid by your benefactor. It wouldn't surprise me if she builds a gallery of contemporary portraiture to house it."

"Ardith is certainly capable of doing that if she deems it necessary. I couldn't believe the museum actually accepted the portrait-sized piece for their Benefactors Gallery," I said. "I've had three inquiries regarding portraits since it was hung."

"Well, it is here on loan for your opening and I wouldn't be surprised if there were other people on the board of directors or who are major benefactors who will contact you at or after the show," Mai Lin said. I had yet to meet the gallery owner face-to-face, though I suspected I'd met her in other ways.

⸓

Rita saw me slip my shoes off at the entry of the gallery and smiled at me. She reached up to adjust my bowtie and brush imaginary lint from my tux.

"I'll keep your shoes where they are safe," she said. "Have you seen the inspiration for your painting?" I looked at her with a brow raised.

168

Would I meet the women with whom I had danced that Sunday morning? Instead, Rita led me to the sculpture. It was the stone version, but I had brought a different image to the canvas. Still, it would be easy for people to draw a comparison between the sculpture and my triptych hanging nearby.

The painting showed the three sisters as flesh emerging from stone, but in reaching toward the viewer a dozen hands emerged as well. It had been impossible to know for certain how many women had been involved in my stone orgy.

"I put it as near the scene of the crime as I could," a voice whispered beside me. I jerked toward her. Her petite Chinese features were reflected in the face of one of the goddesses in the painting. Yet, it was the first time I'd actually been in the presence of the gallery owner. She was a middle-aged bespectacled Asian woman with hair in a tight bun. Her red dress clung to her curves to about mid-calf, but it was slit up the side nearly to her hip. Her high heels added a good three inches to her height.

"I'll check on the refreshments," Rita said as she slipped away. "And let you two get reacquainted." She giggled a little and gave me a peck on the cheek before she hurried away—with my shoes. I turned back to Mai Lin.

"You were there," I whispered.

"Oh, yes. When Rita showed me your art and explained how she had been conducting experiments, I was a willing co-conspirator. And I'm very proud of how you depicted me in the painting. Come, I have something to show you."

I followed Mai Lin to her office. She stopped one of her associates and gave her instructions regarding opening the gallery doors at precisely eight o'clock. "The artist will arrive at eight-thirty."

"Yes, ma'am."

"Even Rita doesn't know I have this," Mai Lin said as we entered her office. "I thought you deserved to look back on what occurred that Sunday morning with a little perspective."

She turned her computer screen toward me and launched a video playback. I was embarrassed when I saw myself, naked, embracing stone statues at the beginning. Mai Lin advanced the video to the point where I began exploring *The Three Sisters*. I'd never seen such an erotic performance in my life. Performance was the only word I could put to it as I saw Rita, Mai Lin, and a third woman I'd never met before become living statues, dancing around me, shedding clothes and inhibitions as they maneuvered me from one to the next. In minutes, while watching this, I found myself stimulated to a powerful erection.

"That looks painful," Mai Lin said softly. I tore my eyes away from the screen to her, only to discover her silk sheath of a dress had been removed. She reached to unfasten my fly and release my straining cock. "Now, watch and remember," she said as she straddled my lap and let my prick slide between her slick nether lips. I raised a hand to stroke her breasts as my eyes returned to the screen. The sensations were multiplied as I watched our quartet on screen and felt her tight pussy clamp down around me.

"This is my favorite part," she said as the scene changed to show me lying back on the marble bench with my head in the lap of a sculpture. In the video, Mai Lin—completely nude now—rose from behind me and flung a leg over me. She was so short, her crotch barely cleared my torso with her feet planted on the floor on either side of me. Rita slipped up behind her and guided my cock into her folds as the third, still unnamed, woman fed me her breast to suckle. Once she was firmly planted on my pole, Mai Lin leaned back into Rita's arms and passionately kissed her as they stroked each other's backs and breasts. I could see on the screen the undulation of Mai Lin's stomach around my cock, just as I could feel it on me now. A growling moan emanated from the woman. I could imagine it in the silent video playing before me and knew I was about to release in climax, just as she did.

The clip came to an end and Mai Lin collapsed against my chest, exhausted from her orgasm, just as I was panting from mine. Her internal muscles continued to clench and spasm around my cock for another minute. At last, she moved back, releasing my prick from her folds to drop wetly against my stomach. She gently leaned forward and sucked me into her mouth, cleaning our spend from my cock and balls.

"I promised you would appear at the exhibit at eight-thirty," she said as she pulled her panties on and dropped the silk sheath over her head. "That leaves us time for just this." She leaned forward and planted a long sensuous kiss on my lips, never even touching me with her tongue. When she pulled back, I was nearly hard again. "Now put that away and save it for Rita later," she said.

———❈———

A crowd had begun to gather in the gallery, most carrying glasses of champagne and looking as elegant as any formal ball. Rita and Kelly moved up on either side of me as I entered the gallery ahead of Mai Lin. They grasped my arms in a hug and leaned in to kiss my cheeks.

"So, there you are," Rita said. "Did Mai Lin have her way with you?" I smiled and was sure I was blushing. "She's been talking about what she was going to do for the past three months. I'm surprised she waited so long!" I kissed my sweetheart, gave Kelly a hug, and began circulating among the guests, accepting a glass of champagne from a server as easily as I accepted the compliments being paid to me. I met a councilman and the chairman of the arts commission. The benefactor who made our orchestra hall possible stopped to ask me about portraits for him and his wife.

As we circulated, I saw a small crowd gathered around the painting of Cold Fusion. I inhaled deeply and went to face the music. As I suspected, Sheila and Harold Monroe were at the center of the small group. Much to my amazement, Sheila was describing exactly how her sitting with me had gone.

"I was exactly as cold as the painting shows," she described. "After I'd come, I told him to hurry up and fuck me, because I had to pick up the children. I couldn't believe he declined."

"I wouldn't have," said a man nearby. "I'd say that ass was worth a frostbit dick." The crowd laughed. I could tell these had to be the

Monroes' inner circle, but I was still surprised Sheila would talk so frankly about the encounter in the presence of her husband. It was, in fact, Harold who noticed my approach first.

"Ah, here's the artist now," Harold said. "I, for one, have always doubted that presented with this lovely ass, he turned away. I think Sheila was so overwhelmed by his prowess, she's embarrassed to talk about it." I didn't know what to think about the man's brashness. He was, as I suspected, a good bit older than Sheila. It must be difficult for a man in his sixties to have children in elementary school. He seemed quite proud of his wife's sexuality, though.

"I'd like to commission a painting like this," said a man I hadn't met. "Of my wife, of course, not me." Everyone laughed.

"I've painted only two commissions in this style and they each took several weeks of sittings and connecting to the model before I was able to complete it. They really can't be commissioned to come out like this. They are what I paint from inspiration, not from contract. The Monroes can certainly show you my portraiture work if you like."

"I'd sit for a portrait, even if there was only a slight chance I would end up in a painting like this," a woman said. I glanced to her and saw she was holding the arm of the man who requested a commission. "I've heard he is so discreet, he never reveals the names of his models." She was tall, almost statuesque, with short blonde hair. Her cocktail dress was cut low in front, showing ample cleavage. Her brown eyes burned into me as she held my gaze. A hint of a smile played at her lips. Slow dawning came upon me. We'd made the connection, but the moment was brief.

"Well, I'm happy to let anyone know the woman in this artwork is my Sheila," Harold boasted. "I've prepared a spot at the end of our bed for this painting and intend to look at it every time I pierce her pussy."

"Christmas and the Fourth of July," snickered Sheila.

"I'd still be interested in the commission," the man with the statuesque blonde said.

"Please discuss that with my lovely assistant Rita," I answered.

I FOUND A woman in a wheelchair in front of the painting of Lori I'd called *Submission*. She was heavy with the weight of years of confinement in the chair. Still, her smile was one of complete satisfaction. She looked up at me and I knelt so we were at eye-level.

"I'm Doc Peters," I said, holding out my hand. She took it lightly but did not return the salutation. She looked back at the painting. "That was a pleasure to paint," I said, rather lamely.

"Her mistress is pleased," the young woman said. My attention was caught by another who approached the other side of the chair. I looked up at Lori Kraft, the model for this piece. She handed the young woman a glass of champagne and smiled at me.

"Pleasing my mistress is all that matters," Lori said.

My attention was called to the other side of the room and I had to excuse myself. I hoped I would learn more about the couple eventually.

I OPENED A package that had just arrived as Rita was talking on the phone a week later. Inside was a book, *On My Own*, the cover of which was the painting I'd done of Donna Barrett. Inside the front cover was an inscription.

> *Doc,*
>
> > *You have known my work and I have known yours. Thank you for my portrait, this book cover, and my wonderful new home. I will always remember posing for you.*
>
> *Donna Barrett*

I showed the book to Rita and she smiled. She finished her telephone conversation and turned to me.

"The Gallery of Modern Art met our reserve bid on *Stone Orgy*. It looks like you have another museum piece in your portfolio!" With the notices on my exhibition, I had skyrocketed to fame as a contemporary artist. Of course, I no longer had any inventory. And no current inspirations. It looked like I'd still be selling real estate at this time next year. If experience told me anything, it was that it would take two years to paint enough pieces for another exhibition.

"It will be a while before I can put together enough pieces for another exhibition. I need to earn a living, too."

"But you could paint full-time now. Quit selling real estate and just paint," Rita said.

"As if it were an 8-5 job?"

"Oh. But… I thought what you really wanted was to just be an artist."

*How can I explain this?*

"Just being an artist doesn't necessarily mean *making a living* from art. That's the trap I fell into before. It's why everything I've done in the past fifteen years was so commercial. It was a job and I earned extra money from it. It wasn't until I went into the studio after my evening with Allison and let my emotions loose—just threw paint at the canvas—that I painted anything significant just because I wanted to paint. I make a living selling real estate and just because I made a year's income from the gallery opening doesn't mean I can quit my day job."

It was still amazing to me, though. The sale of nine paintings in one night, even after commissions, was equal to what I could expect in a normal year's income selling real estate. But I knew better than to act like a lottery winner and just chuck my stable life in favor of being an artiste. It wouldn't be long before I was cranking out commissions at the rate of one or two a month and looking at my art like it was a digital photo.

"Besides," I said, "I don't have any idea what to paint next." And that was the real problem. Of the paintings exhibited at the gallery, each arose from a sexually charged encounter with a woman and most had been arranged by Rita. We'd been lovers for almost two years now. We were living together. Though we'd never discussed our relationship in terms of exclusivity and permanence, I was pretty certain that coming home to find me fucking another woman in what had become 'our bed' would not be looked on kindly. And I was content with that. Rita was more than I ever dreamed possible as a lover, companion, and even business manager.

As if on cue, the doorbell rang. Rita left the studio and I doodled on a pad. There was one other inspiration waiting to be realized. Another from the Sunday among the sculptures. About ten minutes later, Rita and Kelly came into the studio sipping coffee. Rita offered me a cup.

"Hi, Doc!" Kelly said. "Congratulations on the great show."

"I couldn't have done it without your help, Kelly," I said truthfully. *Out of Body* had sold for $22,000. That night had been the first of Rita's experiments.

"Oh, you had lots of models and had already done one painting before I came along," she laughed. She sat on the daybed and Rita cuddled up close to her. *What is she up to?*

"Yes, but it was you joining me on the first experiment that proved my theory that we could create the environment from which art could emerge," Rita said.

"Thank you very much, but I still feel a little guilty. I used both of you that night. Doc as an experimental dildo and an excuse to get into your panties," Kelly said. "I was not very professional in my role as an observer."

"I'd like to dissuade you of that thought," I said. "How can I express how much you've meant in both of our lives?" Rita took Kelly's hand.

"Um… I really appreciate your thought, Doc, but you know I don't really want to do that again. Yours is the only cock that's ever been in my pussy, and the only one that will ever have been there. I'm just not interested in a repeat."

"Nor am I, Kelly," I said. "Well, that's a lie. I confess that anytime you find yourself wanting that stimulation, I'm willing to help out. But that's not what I meant."

"I want another experiment, Kelly," Rita said. "Did you see what Doc was drawing when we came in? He's been obsessed with that image since before the show. He just hasn't been able to get it right. I thought maybe you'd be interested in posing."

"What's the image about?" Kelly asked. I could see her breathing deepen and understood what Rita was doing. I sat at the easel and continued my doodles.

"It's a sculpture that Doc only experienced through his senses other than sight. It's called *Sapphic Kiss*. Of course, because of the subject matter and the fact that he needs to draw, he couldn't be involved in the action."

"When I tried to get involved the first time, her lips were cold and tasted of stone," I added.

"A kiss takes two people," Kelly said, turning her eyes hotly on Rita. "Who would be my partner?"

"You know I'll kiss you anytime," Rita replied. She proved it by pressing her lips to Kelly's.

I drew dozens of sketches, some rapidly and some as if there was just one detail to capture. I moved my stool around to different positions so I could see the scene unfold from different directions. As soon as Kelly realized what we were doing, she became a willing partner. Had I used a video camera instead of paper and pencils, I could have sold it as the hottest new girl-girl porn on the market. I admit, I needed to loosen my trousers in order to release the pressure.

The girls' clothing was pulled aside, but not fully discarded. I could see breasts as they suckled each other and occasionally a pussy with fingers plunging into it. As the two rose toward yet another peak of passion, I moved to the floor. Rita was mostly under Kelly and both women were in the rictus of orgasm.

Then it happened. As their faces relaxed, Kelly lowered her lips to Rita's and they held the kiss, savoring their post-orgasmic connection. "Don't move," I pled in a whisper. I was in position to look up past Rita's face into Kelly's eyes. It was the perfect Sapphic kiss.

By the time they broke their pose and got dressed, I was sketching the details on a canvas and getting ready to paint. I kissed each of them lightly as they left the studio and began mixing the colors on my palette.

⸎

"You have letters of interest from two galleries in New York, one in Chicago, one in Houston, and one in San Francisco," Rita said, removing her very professional looking glasses. I'd been sketching her as she looked through her papers. It was a pose and she held her position with the glasses near her face. Of course, she was nude. Of course. "I know you don't have enough pieces for a full new exhibition, but *Sapphic Kiss* is wonderful and a new starting point after your first showing. We still have five pieces unsold from the show and Mai Lin will be closing it and shipping in two weeks."

"I thought we had six pieces unsold."

"Oh, I forgot to tell you." She had an impish smile on her face that let me know she'd been saving news for the right moment. "*Hecate Rising* has sold."

"Don't tell me Ardith finally decided to build an addition on her house to display it. The piece is huge," I laughed. She was the only person I could think of who would even have an interest. The painting was seven feet tall and four feet wide. I'd been considering adding a room myself to display it.

"Oh, you know how well Ardith is connected. A certain noble in England was recently here for a visit. She arranged a private viewing of your exhibition. He was taken by the portrait and insisted on buying it and having it sent to England to display in his castle."

"My God! It will cost a fortune just to ship the piece!"

"Not just ship it. He wants it framed first and is sending a professional curator to travel with the piece. With the $50,000 purchase price, getting the painting to his castle will cost well over $100,000."

"With the how much purchase price?" Certainly, I hadn't heard her correctly.

"Oh. Did I forget to mention he paid $50,000 for the painting?" Rita was so smug. I laid down my sketch pad and embraced my

177

nymph. She flowed willingly into my arms. I never in my life imagined a painting of mine would sell for $50,000.

I hadn't paid much attention to the sales and prices of the pieces. Rita had taken upon herself the job of acting as personal assistant for my art career. I loved the way she was looking out for me.

"You are amazing!"

"Don't leave Mai Lin out of the thanks. In fact, there are a number of women who have called wanting to model for you. I have a whole bunch of experiments I'd like to try!"

"You have? I rather thought that was just something you did to get me started."

"Oh, it got you started, all right. It got me started, too. My sex life is the envy of the entire whine and dine group."

"You talk about it?"

"Well, a little." Rita had the good sense to blush and lower her eyes. I chuckled and she continued. "You have a portrait scheduled next week that will get you started."

"Who is it with?"

"Megan Frost."

"Do I know her?"

"Statuesque. Short blonde hair. Let's just say one of the three sister goddesses wants another crack at you. I'm betting that in addition to paint fumes, the studio will smell of sex for days and you'll be painting another fantasy."

"You don't mind?" I asked as I planted another kiss on her face.

"I expect some of that smell to be mine."

I lifted her and carried her to the bedroom. She kissed me long and hard, but wasn't finished with her news yet.

"Your models, who now call themselves 'Doc's Atelier,' meet together once a month now to brainstorm experiments they can use to keep you painting. You'll be surprised at the opportunities awaiting you."

I kissed her forehead, her eyes, her nose, and eventually found her lips again. Our lips were made for each other. No matter what other models came into my life, no matter how many joined Doc's Atelier, my lovely assistant Rita would fuel my fantasies for years to come.

---

# The End

# An Interview with author Devon Layne

KEEPING HIS IDENTITIES separate is sometimes a challenge, but author/editor/designer Nathan Everett attacks the challenge of interviewing his alter ego, Devon Layne, with precision borne of living a double life for years. Here's what Devon had to say to Nathan about the publication of the Signature Edition of *The Art and Science of Love*.

**NE:** Devon, you've written a lot of stories about artists, and *The Art and Science of Love* was the first. Who is *your* favorite artist?

**DL:** Oh, that's a surprising question. I'm going to assume you mean of the artists I've written about. I'd say Tony Ames from the *Model Student* series is probably my favorite. I was truly inspired when I wrote his story. Of course, I like Doc Peters in *The Art and Science of Love*, too.

**NE:** Of course. Well, how did the character of Doc Peters come about?

**DL:** It started a long long time ago. I'd say back in about 1996. I was putting together a story about some blackjack players who had a system for winning and created a team that went to Reno to test it. But every member of the team was being blackmailed. The main character who invented the system also lived a life writing erotica on a popular website that was around back then.

I was writing about his secret life and decided I needed to actually write one of his stories in order to have something he could be sued for. It was a story about working with his Lovely Assistant Rita. When I finished writing it, though, I was embarrassed by how explicit the sex was and locked the story with a password that I didn't open for nearly twenty years.

**NE:** Still embarrassed about it?

**DL:** Most of the story shows up here in **The Art and Science of Love**. It inspired me to expand the relationship between Rita and Doc—Doc being the artist and Rita being a 'scientific' investigator of what inspired Doc's best paintings.

**NE:** So not embarrassed?

**DL:** Not really. The sex in this story might be a little more raw than my more recent works, but it's inspiring.

**NE:** So, this is not a new story, even discounting the sealed version from '96. When did you pull it out?

**DL:** Life has a number of little crises that make it interesting. Suffice it to say that the trigger was understanding that my marriage was about to end. That came in 2011, almost two years before the actual termination. *You* had just finished writing **For Money or Mayhem** which has a very hard and emotional ending. *I* felt what was needed at this juncture was something with a happy ending. Nothing has a happier ending than erotica. Remarkably, I remembered the password I used to lock the original file and went to work from there.

**NE:** And this book is the result?

**DL:** Not exactly. I posted the original story on SOL. It was twelve chapters and a little less than 50,000 words. It wasn't until 2020 that I went back and read the story, realizing that I'd left so much out of it. This Signature Edition is the result of that rewrite.

**NE:** Back to where I started this conversation. You write a lot of stories about artists. Why? Are you an artist?

**DL:** Not as such. I dabble in sketching, but I'm not very good at it. I design. I was once a theatrical designer, which is my educational background. But I know that when a creative mood starts in, there is a kind of focus that transcends time and space. I experience it when I'm writing. I just use a thousand words to paint a picture.

**NE:** So, you've written about painters, sculptors, photographers, cooks, and theatrical designers. Why no writers?

**DL:** Yeah. I do spend a lot of time talking about writing in my blog, which has now been going for over a hundred episodes. I feel like I've covered most of the writing process—except for one thing. That's the transcendence of the mood when one is writing. Because I haven't been able to capture that in a blog yet, I'm thinking I will focus on a writer soon. My first new publication of 2025, *Soulmates*, included a young writer, but she wasn't developed as a major character outside the realm of her relationship with the other head talkers. The sequel might be her opportunity to take center stage.

**NE:** I know there was something else you wanted to say about *The Art and Science of Love*. What was it?

**DL:** When I was at the lowest point of my life that I can remember, I started writing erotica with this story. I began posting it online after I had just one chapter written and kept posting a couple of chapters a week. The response I got to that story saved me. I received dozens of emails—maybe hundreds—asking me to please keep writing, and telling me how great I was. That wasn't all it took to bring me out of my depression, of course, but it was a significant contributing factor. When I couldn't give myself affirmations, readers jumped in and affirmed my talent and creativity. I owe the start of my career writing erotica—now over sixty books—to posting this story and the reader response I received. I don't think it is my best writing by any means, but it showed me that people were hungry for what I could produce.

**NE:** We have a few of those comments:

> *"An exceptionally well written little tale."*

> *"Great story. I have really enjoyed reading it."*

> *"I think it's a perfectly wonderful story. Being involved in the arts, I am appreciating his breakthrough in painting."*

*"An incredibly good story. Educational too."*

*"Your story stands heads and shoulders above a number of others because your characters are more developed. To me, it's less important whether I like or dislike them than that I care enough about them to like or dislike them. And I think you succeed in that. Also, while there are sex aplenty, it's a part of the story (that enriches it) and not the ONLY thing in the story."*

*"A unique approach to erotica. I normally skip the non-romantic pieces but yours captivated me. A piece with "romance for the moment" but commitment for a longer spell. Excellent text pictorials without the vulgarity. You use prose like your painter used his brush."*

*"Wow. A piece of erudite, brain-seducing erotica. What a treat. Thanks so much."*

*"I've just been reading your stories and to say I was entertained would be an understatement. I felt as though I was part of the story. I could imagine the colour of the brush strokes but also enjoy the erotic pleasure. I must admit I was quite envious of the artist."*

**DL:** Is it too late to blush?
**NE:** Congratulations on another *Signature Edition*.